Renew by phone or online
0845 0020 777

'I enjoyed being with you this evening, *carissima*,' he told her, tucking a strand of hair back behind her ear, his fingers lingering, caressing her baby-soft skin.

'Rico...'

Uncertainty wavered in her voice. He looked into stunning sage-green eyes, seeing the dawning awareness in their depths before his gaze dropped to her mouth. The temptation was too much. He could not resist another second.

'I have to kiss you.' Her eyes widened in response to his husky, needy appeal, and he felt the tremor that ran through her. Conscious of her wariness, and determined to build the trust between them, he tried to rein in his urgent hunger and asked her to make the decision—praying she would agree. 'May I, Ruth?'

Dear Reader

It was always my intention that Ruth would one day get to tell her own story as part of my ongoing series of Strathlochan books. What I had not anticipated at the start was that Rico Linardi would ever reappear. But he swiftly became a special character for me—an unforgettable and sexy hero who demanded his own story!

It was also obvious that Rico was the perfect man for beautiful, over-achieving, workaholic GP Ruth Baxter. Ruth who has never known love and who has been so hurt in the past. In consequence, she has immersed herself in work, while deep inside what she really craves is to be accepted, to be good enough, to belong.

An unexpected turn of events brings Rico and Ruth face to face. It's a life-changing moment for them both. Can Rico teach Ruth to trust—in herself and in him—and to believe in a once-in-a-lifetime love?

I hope you will enjoy Rico and Ruth's story, which is the ninth of my loosely linked Scottish Medical™ Romances.

Love

Margaret
www.margaretmcdonagh.com

ITALIAN DOCTOR, DREAM PROPOSAL

BY
MARGARET McDONAGH

First published in Great Britain 2009
Large Print edition 2010
Harlequin Mills & Boon Limited,
Eton House, 18-24 Paradise Road,
Richmond, Surrey TW9 1SR

© Margaret McDonagh 2009

ISBN: 978 0 263 21077 4

Printed and bound in Great Britain
by CPI Antony Rowe, Chippenham, Wiltshire

Margaret McDonagh says of herself: 'I began losing myself in the magical world of books from a very young age, and I always knew that I had to write, pursuing the dream for over twenty years, often with cussed stubbornness in the face of rejection letters! Despite having numerous romance novellas, short stories and serials published, the news that my first "proper book" had been accepted by Harlequin Mills & Boon for their Medical™ Romance line brought indescribable joy! Having a passion for learning makes researching an involving pleasure, and I love developing new characters, getting to know them, setting them challenges to overcome. The hardest part is saying goodbye to them, because they become so real to me. And I always fall in love with my heroes! Writing and reading books, keeping in touch with friends, watching sport and meeting the demands of my four-legged companions keeps me well occupied. I hope you enjoy reading this book as much as I loved writing it.'

www.margaretmcdonagh.com
margaret.mcdonagh@yahoo.co.uk

Praise for Medical™ Romance author Margaret McDonagh:

'This is such a beautiful, wonderfully told
and poignant story that I truly didn't want it to end.
Margaret McDonagh is an exceptional writer
of romantic fiction, and with
VIRGIN MIDWIFE, PLAYBOY DOCTOR
she will tug at your heartstrings, make you cry,
and leave you breathless!'
—*The Pink Heart Society Reviews*

'Romance does not get any better than this!
Margaret McDonagh is a writer readers
can always count on to deliver a story that's poignant,
emotional and spellbinding, and
AN ITALIAN AFFAIR is no exception!'
—*CataRomance.com*

ACKNOWLEDGEMENTS

Many thanks are due to the following:

Michael and Kate Dann
www.michaeldann.co.uk

John and the
Primary Immunodeficiency Association
www.pia.org.uk

and Dr Nick Edwards
author of "In Stitches"…

for their help with my research for this book

And to:

Mara
for keeping my Italian
on the straight and narrow

Fiona, Lesley, Jennifer, Jackie,
Christine and Irene for their patience,
encouragement, care and support

and most especially to
Jo, my wonderful editor,
without whom none of this would be possible

CHAPTER ONE

DR RUTH BAXTER breathed a sigh of relief as she arrived at her destination, even though the only empty space she could find in the car park was the one furthest away from the hotel's main entrance. Having got up at stupid o'clock—after a scant few hours' sleep following two patient callouts during her Sunday night as on-duty GP—the journey had taken longer than expected thanks to heavy Monday-morning traffic and a lengthy hold-up after an accident on the M6 motorway. All of which meant she was now late for the two-day medical conference she was here to attend.

Ruth picked up her briefcase and overnight bag, locked her car, and headed towards the hotel. Currently bathed in warm May sunshine, the impressive building stood in its own grounds and overlooked the glittering expanse of Morecambe Bay. The lovely weather was a welcome change from the grey skies she had left behind in Strathlochan—not to mention the torrential rain she had encountered once she had crossed the Scotland/England border and had skirted the edge of the Lake District on the motorway.

As she walked, Ruth reflected on the last month and the events that had brought her here. Immunology was a field of medicine she had known little about until the arrival of a new patient had set her on an unexpected journey of discovery. Instinct had led her to the Internet where her research had uncovered papers written by Dr Riccardo Linardi, a world-renowned immunologist and allergist.

She had emailed Dr Linardi about her patient and, despite the many demands on his time, he had responded at once, his detailed advice proving to be invaluable. Instead of ending there, as Ruth had expected it to, their email correspondence had increased, widening to discussions on immunology and allergies in general. When he'd told her he was speaking at this conference and had invited her to attend as his guest, Ruth had been amazed and delighted.

Dr Linardi knew she was based in the UK, and she knew he was flying in from America, but that was the extent of their exchange of personal information. Now they were to meet. And the implication had hovered, unmentioned, that this could become a kind of informal interview. A testing of the waters for both of them. For now she was keeping an open mind, and her feet on the ground, waiting to see how the next two days played out. Who knew what opportunities might lie ahead?

Entering the hotel, Ruth crossed the spacious lobby to the reception desk, where the clerk welcomed her with a warm smile before informing her that she had, indeed, missed the meet-and-greet welcome breakfast.

'The first session of the conference has just started, but you are by no means the last to arrive, Dr Baxter. Several other delegates have also reported delays,' the clerk reassured her as Ruth signed in. 'May I arrange for your luggage to be taken to your bedroom? That way you can head straight to the conference.'

'Thank you.'

Smiling, Ruth accepted the efficient young woman's suggestion and pocketed her room key. Keeping her briefcase, she took the name badge and conference schedule the clerk gave her, then followed the directions to the adjacent extension where the conference was being held. It seemed ages since the banana and hasty cup of coffee she had managed to grab before leaving home, but further shots of caffeine would now have to wait until the mid-morning break.

Trying to stem the nervousness that always assailed her when facing people she didn't know, Ruth took a deep breath and stepped inside, closing the door quietly behind her. She found herself at the side and near the front of the large room. The two-hundred-plus delegates sat listening to the grey-haired, bespectacled man who was talking into the microphone. Behind him on the platform was a line of several speakers and officials, and nearby was a display screen which currently depicted a super-sized illustration of the virus under discussion.

Spotting an empty chair at the end of the third row from the front, and hoping not to be noticed, or to disturb the speaker, Ruth tiptoed towards it. Once settled in her place, she wondered if the bespectacled older man still at the microphone was Dr Linardi. She suspected not, given the old-school opinions he was sharing with the audience, opinions that were way out of sync with those expressed in his emails to her. There was also the absence of any identifiable accent, American or otherwise.

Ruth suppressed a smile. It was unlike her to indulge in fancy, yet she had built up an image of 'her' Dr Linardi these last few weeks. In her mind he was a middle-aged, avuncular figure, not exactly a caricature of the archetypal mad professor but certainly a paternal, kind, possibly slightly eccentric man who was respected by his peers, his students and his patients alike.

Opening the conference programme, Ruth noted that, as well as holding a two-hour workshop that afternoon and giving the final talk that would bring the conference to a close on Tuesday afternoon, Dr Linardi was also scheduled to speak next, right before the mid-morning break. Anxiety, excitement and expectation welled inside her. Soon she would see and hear the man who had made a big impact on her life this last month and who, quite possibly, could play a major role in her future.

She had no idea what might lie ahead but there was no turning back now.

Dr Riccardo Linardi sat on the raised dais at the front of the conference room, stifling a yawn as the first speaker continued his talk. After a two-month tour of lectures and consultations in North America he was tired, Rico conceded.

Mentally weary. And longing for home. However, he had commitments to fulfil before he could return to Italy, one of which had brought him to this hotel on England's Lancashire coast.

He had complicated matters by asking Dr Ruth Baxter to attend this conference, but she had impressed him from the moment her first email had arrived seeking guidance about her patient. The one hundred or more disorders that came under the category of primary immunodeficiency often went undiagnosed and were difficult to spot. Which was why he had been so surprised that Ruth, apparently a young and relatively inexperienced GP, had not only recognised what several more senior doctors had missed but had backed her intuition and pursued the matter with single-minded determination.

Ruth's thirst for knowledge and enquiring mind had grabbed his attention, and he had continued their correspondence over the last month. The amount she had learned in a short time amazed him. He came across few people with such instinctive and innate talent as that which Ruth had displayed. If, in person, she lived up to his expectations, he would definitely offer her a job.

Catching movement from the corner of his eye, Rico turned his head in time to notice the door at the side of the room open. His weariness was forgotten as his attention became riveted on the woman who entered. She closed the door and paused for a moment before trying to slip unnoticed to a vacant chair at the end of the third row right in front of him.

But Rico noticed. How could he not? She was stunning. In her mid- to late twenties, he guessed, she was coolly beautiful. Elegant and graceful. Polished. Not in a flashy way but with a natural style and class. Left loose, her blonde hair fell to her shoulder blades in a pale gold curtain. It shone with health and looked silky soft. His fingers itched to run through the satin strands, and he imagined how they would look fanned out across his pillow or feel feathering across his bare skin.

He tried to rein in his wayward thoughts, to turn away and ignore the woman who had immediately intrigued him. It proved impossible. He had neither the time nor inclination for a dalliance, however pleasurable, yet his disobedient gaze lingered, appraised, admired. He was just looking, he reassured himself. That was all. It didn't mean he was going to do anything about it—even if it had been far longer than he cared to admit since he'd been with a woman.

Giving in to temptation, Rico tuned out the speaker and gave the woman the attention and appreciation she deserved. As she approached the vacant chair, he could tell she was above average height and was wearing shoes with an almost flat heel. She would be the perfect fit for his own six-foot frame.

The slate-grey trousers that encased long, long legs were impeccably tailored, fitting her to per-fection, hinting at her womanly curves rather than clinging to them, teasing and tempting rather than being obvious. She slipped off the matching jacket and turned to hang it over the back of the chair. The hem of her long-sleeved, dark green jumper brushed the gentle swell of her hips, riding up slightly as she bent to untangle the jacket, allowing him a brief glimpse of her delectable derrière before she turned round again.

His gaze roamed upwards. The jumper's cashmere fabric hugged the slight indentation of her waist, then moulded to the shape of her breasts—breasts that were not big but were natural and exquisitely formed. Just the right size to fill his palms. Rico sucked in a ragged breath, his body tightening with a rush of desire. He clenched hands that itched to caress her firm softness, shifting on his chair to mask his discomfort.

As the woman sat down, Rico noted that the demure neckline of her top served only to highlight the graceful line of her throat. Her jawline was feminine, although the tilt of her chin betrayed a hint of stubborn determination. Rosy and tempting, her mouth was designed for kissing, with a plump lower lip and an appealingly bowed top one. Her nose was straight, her cheekbones high, while her brows—a few shades darker than her hair—arched neatly above her eyes. From this distance he could not determine their colour but he guessed they would be blue. He looked forward to a break in conference proceedings so that he could get close enough to her to find out.

She looked up, a slight frown on her face as she glanced around the room. The way even white teeth nibbled at her lower lip not only had his gut clenching in response but also betrayed a nervousness endearingly at odds with her outward composure. Filled with a sense of heated anticipation, Rico waited as she scanned the row of speakers on the platform to his left. He held his breath as, one by one, she moved closer.

Finally, her gaze clashed with his—and held. Rico saw her eyes widen and her lips part in a gasp, but he was too busy trying to contend with his own fierce reaction to assess or worry about hers. All the air had been squeezed from his lungs and his heart was pounding, sending his blood careening through his veins.

He felt as if he had been hit with a sledgehammer or zapped with an electrically charged thunderbolt. Probably both at once. The eye contact sparked an immediate, intense connection, unlike anything he had experienced before. He had known attraction in the past, even basic lust, but all that paled into insignificance given what was happening now. Nothing had prepared him for this shocking, incredible moment of recognition, of knowing he wanted her, *needed* her, had to have her…that she was *the one*.

Dio mio!

Maybe lack of sleep was causing his mind to play tricks on him. There had to be some reasonable explanation for this madness. He was an intelligent man, a scientist. He dealt in facts, in reality, in logic, not in some inexplicable and implausible flight of whimsy. But their private moment of connection continued and neither of them was able to look away. Rico felt as if time was suspended, as if they were somehow being locked together by invisible bonds. Everything around him faded to a blur. He could hear nothing but the rush of blood in his ears, could see nothing but the vision a few feet away, was aware of nothing and no one but her.

Why here? Why now? How could it happen out of the blue like this? How could one look throw his whole world into confusion? Who *was* this woman playing havoc with his senses?

Rico had no answers. Not yet. But soon he would find out everything he needed to know about the mysterious woman who so unexpectedly touched something deep inside him. He did not understand it, but neither did he question it, because he knew it had happened to his father, and he had seen it happen to his cousin. Now, for the first time, Rico truly understood how they had felt. Because he was feeling it, too. When he was least prepared, and when he had thought it might never happen to him, he had found *her*.

He was all too aware that many obstacles lay ahead. Yet one look at her had been enough to know this was it…and to bring his libido raging back to life after a long hibernation. Holding her gaze, he felt the crackle of electricity zinging back and forth between them.

Impatience gripped him. It was the wrong time and the wrong place. And he never allowed anything to distract him from his work. But right now he longed to forget this conference, Dr Baxter and his responsibilities. Instead, he wanted to gather up this woman and take her away from all these people so they could get to know each other in private and see where this incredible connection took them.

The sound of the chairman thanking the first speaker and asking for questions from the floor impinged on Rico's consciousness, but he still did not break the eye contact that made him feel so charged and aware. Soon it would be time for him to speak. If he could remember how to string two words together. Then would come the first refreshment break. It could not come soon enough. He needed to meet the woman who had just changed his life.

A shiver rippled through Ruth as she sensed that she was being watched. Looking up, she cast a surreptitious glance around the room, but everyone appeared to be focused on the speaker. Nibbling her lower lip, she switched her gaze to the platform. Starting with the person furthest away from her, she moved one by one along the row until she reached the man on the nearest end, in line with her, only to find herself staring into a pair of intense dark eyes, eyes that seemed to devour her, looking at her with…what?

From this distance Ruth wasn't sure, but whatever it was it scared the life out of her. A gasp escaped unchecked before her breath lodged in her lungs. Her heart thudded unnaturally fast under her ribs and the room suddenly seemed far too hot. Everything and everyone around her faded from her consciousness. All she could see was *him*. Panic welled within her as she struggled to make sense of the overwhelming surge of emotions now assailing her. Principal amongst them was unfamiliar yet recognisable—desire. Alarmed, she tried to deny it, to banish it, but it refused to go away.

She had given up on men, Ruth reminded herself. Her only serious relationship had been at medical school. It had ended in acrimony, with Adam, a fellow student doctor, leaving her in no doubt about her many deficiencies as a woman. Since then she had never met a man who had remotely stirred her interest to try again and she had been happy to remain alone. In her albeit limited experience, sex was vastly overrated and not worth the effort. Which only served to confirm that the hurtful things Adam had said at the moment of their final parting were true.

Feeling ashamed and humiliated, she had determined never to get involved with a man again, the experience cementing her disbelief in love and romance. At least for herself. Now all that mattered in her life was her work. The only desire that bloomed inside her was to be the best doctor possible for her patients.

So why had one glimpse of *this* man made her feel hotter than Hades? Why was her body betraying her as everything female in her responded to him, causing all her previously redundant hormones to spring to life? Even the dozen or so feet of floor space that separated them failed to lessen his impact or temper the searing force of his gaze.

Something about the man and the way he looked at her made her tremble with awareness and caused an aching knot to tighten deep inside her. She couldn't comprehend the potent affect he had on her. The immediate and uncharacteristic rush of arousal and blaze of sexual hunger were completely beyond her experience or understanding.

In his early thirties, she judged, and younger

than the rest of the people on the platform, the man was impossibly gorgeous. He had the kind of roguish, bad-boy edge about him that gave mothers the vapours and caused fathers to lock up their daughters and throw away the key. Everything about him oozed wickedness and sinful sensuality...warning enough, if any were needed, that he was far too much man for an inept novice like her to handle. Not that she had any intention of *handling* him. No way.

Untamed, his dark hair was thick and over-long, brushing over the collar of his shirt almost to his shoulders, a few strands flopping across his forehead. The few days' growth of stubble that enhanced the masculine set of his jawline added to his rakish good looks and made him appear more like some latter-day buccaneer than a respectable doctor. Those compelling eyes regarded her steadily. Another tingle feathered down her spine. It felt as if he were holding her captive, casting some kind of spell over her from which she would never escape. She had no idea what was happening to her but she sensed its importance, feared the consequences, and wanted to follow every instinct of self-preservation that was crying out for her to run away. But she couldn't move, couldn't break the connection between them.

Ruth was dimly aware of the first speaker taking questions from the delegates, but it was too much effort to concentrate on what was being said. All her energies and focus were centred on the man in front of her. She sensed the very real danger he posed. Somehow she had to avoid him. When everyone rose for the first break, she would find Dr Linardi, have her talk with him, thank him for his help, and then make an excuse to leave early. Then she would hightail it back to Strathlochan and the safety of home.

It was only when the chairman introduced the man she had come here to meet that Ruth was able to wrest her gaze free. Her pulse was racing in response to the intensity of the last few moments. And her hands had clenched so tightly that her short, neatly manicured nails had left crescent-moon indentations in her palms. Feeling vulnerable, her senses heightened, she waited to see who rose to their feet as the chairman handed the stage over to Dr Riccardo Linardi.

Seconds ticked by.

Then…finally…there was movement.

Ruth froze in horror as *he* stood up.

No!

This was *not* the man she had been emailing,

the man who had made her feel valued, and with whom she had agreed to spend the next two days. It couldn't be. And yet some inner part of her had recognised the danger he posed and the life-changing affect he could have on her.

Feeling light-headed with shock, she watched him walk to the microphone with deceptively lazy strides and the cat-like grace of a hunter. And then he spoke, introducing himself in perfect English but with a lilting Italian accent. A wave of fearful desire surged through her as the rich timbre of his voice electrified every nerve-ending in her body.

He briefly scanned the room, then that mesmerising gaze inexorably found her once more, calling to her, claiming her, binding her to him. Terrified, she trembled as she absorbed the enormity of what was happening. This man had jolted her out of her safe cocoon and rocked the very foundations of her world.

Ruth didn't know what to do.

Go…or stay and face the dangerously exciting possibilities that lay ahead?

CHAPTER TWO

'MAY I pour you some coffee, *signorina*? Or would you prefer tea?'

Ruth had not needed to hear the question, delivered in that knee-weakening, huskily accented voice, to know that Dr Linardi had moved up beside her in the informal queue at the self-service refreshment table. She had felt his approach. Every atom of her being was attuned to him. Had been since the moment their gazes had first met.

His talk had been mind-blowing, displaying the breadth of knowledge and passion for the subject that had been so evident in his emails. He had inspired and enthralled her then but even more so in person. Once she had overcome the shock of him, and their inexplicable connection, she had forced herself to focus on her notes. In part because it stopped her looking at him. So she had written copiously, struggling to put the sound of his voice and what it did to her out of her mind. She'd already learned so much over the last month, and listening to Dr Linardi's talk only made her more fascinated with the often obscure and puzzling worlds of allergy and immunology.

That she was also fascinated by the man himself, Ruth tried to ignore. But she had been aware every moment of him watching her. And the knowledge that they would soon meet face to face, that she would most likely be alone with him later in the day, had brought back the urge to run, as if for her very life. He was going to turn her whole world upside down. She knew it. Was scared of it. But she hadn't been able to move a muscle to save herself.

What shocked and puzzled her was that a traitorous part of her didn't want to escape…wanted, instead, to discover where this blaze of attraction might lead. That it should be Dr Linardi who had caused reactions and responses she had never experienced before made things all the more complicated. What if he *did* offer her a job? Could she work with him if every time she saw him or heard his voice she felt the burn of desire? She couldn't imagine he would want an employee who acted like a teenager going through her first crush.

Dr Linardi had been waylaid by several people as he had attempted to leave the stage and head in her direction at the start of the mid-morning break. Thankful for the temporary reprieve, Ruth had slipped on her jacket and, leaving her brief-case under her chair as other people had done, she had gone in search of the refreshments. Feeling nervous, self-conscious and incredibly confused, she had needed as much time as possible to compose herself. All the while she had known there would be no escape, had sensed that he was closing in on her—stalking her as a hunter did its prey.

Now he had caught her and he was waiting for her answer. Unable to resist the magnetic pull, she turned her head and met the full force of that compelling gaze. 'Thank you. Coffee, please.' She silently cursed herself, feeling like a tongue-tied schoolgirl rather than a thirty-year-old doctor.

'Milk and sugar?'

'A splash of milk but no sugar,' she managed, finding the mundane nature of their first actual encounter bizarre given the frighteningly real electric current that flowed back and forth between them.

Half turned away from him as they waited in line at the table, Ruth found herself hemmed in and jostled by the press of other delegates as someone in the line tried to manoeuvre out, carrying a tray of cups and saucers. As she lost her balance, Dr Linardi's arm came out to steady her, an instinctive gesture of protection as he moved to place himself between her and the crowd. The action brought her even closer to him. So close that when she drew in a shaky breath she caught a teasing hint of his scent. Cedar. She recognised it thanks to her best friend Gina's interest in essential oils. On him, the aroma was warm and exotic, masculine and arousing, heightening her awareness of him. Even more disturbing was the way the touch of his palm resting on her hip seemed to brand her right through her clothes.

'You are all right?' he asked with evident concern.

'Yes. Thank you.'

He hesitated, and they shared another moment of silent connection before he released her and turned to busy himself with their drinks. Ruth exhaled a shaky breath, feeling unaccountably light-headed. She pressed one hand to her throat, feeling every throb of her pulse against her palm. Up close he was imposing…six feet of impressive, male perfection. Unable to look away from him, she watched as he filled two cups with fresh, richly scented coffee, adding milk to one and a teaspoon of sugar to the other.

He had nice hands, she noted, well cared for, capable and dexterous. He wasn't wearing a wedding ring and there was no tell-tale paler band of skin to betray that he had ever worn one. The sleeves of his pale blue shirt had been turned up to the elbows, revealing leanly muscled forearms, the olive-toned skin dusted with dark hairs. A functional watch with a plain black strap circled his left wrist. Nothing flashy or ostentatious for this man. Her gaze slid upwards. He wasn't wearing a tie and the top couple of buttons of his shirt were open, allowing a view of the strong column of his throat. Again her gaze roved on, over his handsome profile, just as he turned his head and caught her assessing him.

Ruth felt warmth bloom across her cheeks. Then he smiled, and she feared she might melt into a puddle at his feet. Gentle laughter lines crinkled at the corners of his eyes and the hint of a dimple teased his right cheek, adding to his roguish appeal. Being so gorgeous ought to be illegal. Once more her gaze locked with his and, close to, she discovered that his eyes were an unusual dark hazel with intriguing speckles of gold in them. And they were fringed by the kind of thick, long lashes women yearned for—or paid to imitate—but which in no way softened his overwhelming masculinity.

'Come, *signorina*, let us find somewhere away from this melee to enjoy our coffee and talk.'

Trying to ignore the effect the sound of his voice had on her, Ruth accepted the cup and saucer he gave her, fearing she would spill her drink because her hands were shaking so much. As he drew her away from the milling throng and the noise of myriad simultaneous conversations, he smiled and exchanged greetings with several people, but refused to allow them to detain him. His hand settled possessively at the base of her spine, keeping her close to him and guiding her through an open door and into a small, empty side room where a few tables and chairs had been laid out. Ruth set down her coffee and undid the button on her jacket, thanking him as he solicitously drew out a chair for her to sit down before pulling his own chair nearer to her.

'We have not been properly introduced. I am Dr Riccardo Linardi. But my friends call me Rico.' He rested one arm on the table as he faced her. 'I feel that you and I are going to become very close friends.'

Wondering quite *how* close, Ruth took a fortifying sip of her coffee. As she leaned forward to replace her cup back on its saucer, her jacket parted, revealing the name badge pinned on her jumper. She saw his gaze follow the movement but, before she could speak, shocked surprise registered on his face.

'*You* are Dr Ruth Baxter?' Incredulity laced his voice, while the possessive nature of his next words stunned her and made her pulse race. '*My* Ruth?'

It took Rico a moment to recover from the initial amazement that this woman, who had all but brought him to his knees from the first moment he had looked at her, was the woman he had been emailing for a month, the woman he had invited here in the hope she would accept his offer of a job. *His Ruth.* The coincidence did not escape him. Rico didn't know how it had happened, but it was destiny. Fate. They had been meant to meet.

There was nothing remotely scientific about the knowledge, but deep inside Rico knew it was true—knew that the special moment of recognition that had happened first to his father and then to Seb when they had met their future wives had now happened to him. Ruth was his dream woman come to life, the one he had been waiting for. Not that he could tell her that. Not yet. She would think he was crazy. And she was already edgy. More than once he'd sensed her urge to flee. Thankfully she was still here, but if he handled things badly at this early stage, he would spook her. They needed to get to know each other and for Ruth to feel comfortable with him. Not easy in this setting. And discovering her identity was an unexpected twist that added hugely to the complications that lay ahead. He would need to consider those. But for now, conscious of where they were, he needed to keep things as professional as possible until they had the opportunity to be alone.

Waiting was not going to be easy, however, so he allowed himself a few moments to study her and drink in all the details that were revealed now he was close to her. Nervousness and bewilderment were reflected in the eyes that shyly observed him—eyes that were not blue, as he had predicted, but a beautiful sage green.

She looked adorably flustered by what was happening and also a little scared. The former brought a welling of affectionate amusement, but the latter concerned him. Her inexperience had been obvious immediately and he was astonished by it. Unlike most other women he had met, women who knew how to use their wiles to get what they wanted and had no compunction about doing so, Ruth seemed not to have any understanding of her own appeal.

Ruth was like a breath of fresh air, with no artifice about her, no game playing, no hidden agenda. Instead she displayed an unusual innocence for someone with all her attributes, intelligence and maturity. She had a natural, understated beauty yet was genuinely unaware of it, just as she had no clue about her own sensuality and desirability. And she appeared mystified and more than a little unnerved by the intense mutual attraction they shared. Which only intrigued him more. Ruth was a puzzle, a mass of contrasts. He couldn't wait to unravel all her secrets and to discover how she could be so competent and authoritative in her professional life but seem all at sea in terms of social interaction.

It was unsurprising that Ruth seemed overwhelmed. He certainly was. He'd never experienced anything like this in his life and he was still struggling to make sense of the suddenness of it. Not to mention the urgency of the desire, the desperate need to keep her close.

There were many issues to be faced and overcome, Rico acknowledged, but he was determined that no matter how unexpected, and how inconvenient the timing, having found Ruth, he was going to do everything he could not to lose her again. Careful not to rush her, knowing they both needed time to make sense of what was happening, he curbed his impatience to ask the thousand and one questions bubbling within him and gave her a few moments' peace to drink her coffee and compose herself.

The couple of times he had managed to be close to her he had enjoyed the subtle scent of lavender and sweet sexy woman, a combination unique to Ruth that aroused and excited him, and to which he was already addicted. As he watched, sunlight spilled through the window beside them and reflected on Ruth's hair, making it shine like a halo of pale gold around her face. Just looking at her took his breath away. She was amazing. If this was how Seb had felt when first meeting his special woman, it was no wonder his cousin had been so tied up in knots. Having seen what Seb had been through eight months ago, Rico hoped he had learned enough from his cousin's experiences not to make the same mistakes in his as yet unplanned campaign to win Ruth.

The buzz of awareness and charge of desire were ever-present, but he also felt edgy with tension, knowing he was stepping into the unknown. He was in danger of breaking all his rules about any kind of involvement with a colleague...or potential colleague. But the rules he had lived by until now went out of the window when faced with the reality and the temptation of Ruth. He had never felt like this before, had never experienced this rush of emotion and out-of-control need. Somehow he had to find a way to reconcile work life and private life because now that Fate had delivered Ruth to him, he was not letting her go.

Pushing his coffee aside, no longer needing the caffeine as Ruth was the only stimulant he required, he indulged in studying her. If she wore any make-up at all, it was done with such a light touch it was unnoticeable. There was nothing worse in his opinion than kissing a woman and getting a mouthful of gunk, of tasting powder and grease instead of her sweetness. That would not happen with Ruth. Close up he could see that a faint dusting of freckles was scattered across her cheekbones and the bridge of her nose, and her skin was flawless, almost translucent, incredibly fair.

He was relieved to see no wedding or engagement ring on her finger, but confirming there was no one in her life at the moment was a top priority. Aside from the delicate platinum chain around her neck—her jumper hiding whatever was suspended from it—and the inexpensive watch on her right wrist, she wore no adornment. She didn't need any.

Rico was disappointed as the other tables began to fill up around them and their moment of seclusion was lost. He wanted to keep Ruth all to himself. But several people stopped to speak to him and it was some minutes before he could politely extract himself and return his full attention to her.

'I am sorry, *cara*. If we are visible here we will not be able to avoid interruptions,' he told her with a mix of apology and frustration.

'It's all right.' Her smile was shy and tentative but so pure it sucked the air from his lungs and left him feeling as if he had been punched in the gut. 'I'm sure you're in demand and lots of people will want to discuss things with you. Events like this must give you the chance to catch up with colleagues and exchange views on the run.'

Relieved she was relaxing a little, Rico nodded in agreement, enjoying the sound of her voice, which was melodious yet throaty, her English tones clear and refined, and without an identifiable regional accent. 'You are my guest, Ruth, and my time is devoted to you. These days conferences are thankfully shorter and more focused than they used to be as we are all too busy to be away from our posts for long.'

'You must have a full list of patients awaiting you in America,' she suggested, demonstrating how much they had yet to discover about each other.

'Not in America.' He paused a moment, thanking the waitress who came to clear away their cups and saucers. 'I was there for a few weeks giving lectures and training sessions, as well as consulting on a couple of cases, but my home and my clinic are in Italy.'

'Oh! I didn't realise. When you said you were flying in from New York, I assumed that was where you were based.'

Before he could explain, a German colleague wanted to exchange a few words about the workshop Rico was leading that afternoon. Instead of the enjoyment he normally felt in being able to meet up and talk shop with fellow doctors, now it was impatience that gripped him.

He wanted everyone to go away so that he could have time alone with Ruth. But he was destined to be thwarted. For now.

The temptation to escape and miss the rest of the programme was great, but he couldn't yet succumb to the urgent desire to forget everything else and carry Ruth off to bed. Not only did he have his own commitments but it was important for Ruth to learn and absorb as much as she could, both in terms of increasing her knowledge and being able to make a decision on whether or not to consider a change of direction in her career. However difficult, it was work first and pleasure second—when he had worked out a plan to win her trust and her heart.

'There is much we don't yet know about each other,' he said when they were left alone again. 'I am looking forward to learning all about you, but unfortunately I will have to wait a little longer.' He smiled, noting the mix of anxiety and anticipation that warred in her expression. 'We will have time when conference business has finished for the day—I'm sure we can slip away a bit early. But there is much for us to discuss on a professional level.'

'Pippa Warren,' Ruth ventured, mentioning the eight-year-old girl whose illness had been the catalyst, causing Ruth to email him in the first place.

'Indeed, yes. Sadly her situation is far from rare. I learn about cases of delayed or incorrect diagnoses all too often, both in adults and children. And, with the latter, there are parents who are often at the end of their tether, with no idea which way to turn,' he explained, momentarily distracted by the shimmering colours as Ruth nodded her head and her pale gold hair glinted in the sunlight.

'That was certainly how Pippa's mother Judith appeared when I first met her,' Ruth agreed, a tiny frown knotting her brow. 'She had been passed from pillar to post for several years, with various doctors insisting that Pippa was fine and telling Judith that she was fussing unnecessarily and an over-anxious mother.'

Rico heard similar stories far too frequently. 'A mother's instinct should never be dismissed out of hand. Judith and Pippa struck gold the day they walked into your surgery,' he praised, seeing the hint of a blush colour her cheeks.

'I don't know about that.'

'I do,' he insisted, refusing to let her play down her achievements. 'Many doctors, including those with far more experience than you, would not have recognised what you did, never mind follow it through with such tenacity.'

Looking embarrassed, she shrugged. 'I was just lucky.'

'Luck had nothing to do with it,' Rico chastised, determined that she acknowledge what she had done for Pippa and her mother. 'You are a special doctor, Ruth. And equally as important as your academic excellence is that you really care about your patients. You listen to them and you give them your time—not easy given the pressures doctors are under and the limited period alloted to each consultation. But you go the extra mile, just as you demonstrated with Judith and Pippa. Whereas many others had taken the easy way out—treating only what they saw on the surface, or simply not understanding the relevance of the history and range of symptoms because of lack of training and knowledge—you trusted your instincts and you didn't give up until you had solved the puzzle. And, with immunology, making a diagnosis is often a case of detective work, of sticking in there and not giving up. You did that, Ruth. On your own. I think—in fact, I *know*—that you are amazing.'

'Thank you.'

Two little words and yet they revealed so much, especially an inner aloneness that tightened a knot in his stomach and made him want to pull her into his arms and hug her tight. Her smile was tremulous, while the emotion in her voice, and the expression in eyes glimmering with a suspicion of unshed tears, brought the instinctive knowledge that support *of* her and belief *in* her had been in short supply in the past. He didn't yet know why, but he intended to find out. And then he would ensure that she knew her own worth in the future.

'Where do things stand with Pippa now?' he asked, forcing himself to keep things professional.

'We are waiting for the hospital appointment to come through. I saw Judith last week and she has lots of questions about what will happen when Pippa goes for assessment, and what is involved if the consultant confirms that it is CVID.' It was through Rico's help that Ruth had been able to determine that common variable immunodeficiency or CVID, was the most likely diagnosis. She paused, tucking a strand of hair back behind her ear, an endearing knot of consideration creasing her brow. 'I've tried to reassure her as best I can, but I can't answer everything for her.'

'Have Pippa's symptoms improved at all?' he asked, happy to help Ruth set Judith and Pippa's minds at rest about what might lie ahead for them.

'There has been a small lessening in the severity of some of the symptoms now she has started the broad-spectrum antibiotics you recommended,' Ruth told him, gratitude evident in her smile. 'After her years of recurring infections and other problems, I'm hoping that there hasn't been any permanent damage and that she hasn't developed bronchiectasis.'

Rico nodded as Ruth expressed her worries about the chronic condition that caused widening and scarring of the structures of the bronchi, or breathing tubes. It was one of his concerns for Pippa, too. 'You said that the blood tests showed low levels of serum immunoglobins.'

'That's right. Very low.' She glanced at him, then away again, but not before he had noted the flash of indecision in her eyes. A small sigh escaped and she seemed to be wrestling with something, but before he could question her, she grimaced and began speaking again. 'I had a few problems getting the blood tests done.'

'How do you mean?' Rico frowned.

'They are not tests that would usually be requested from a general practice surgery.'

Rico's frown deepened. 'You had trouble from the hospital when you asked for the tests? Or from your own practice?'

'Questions were asked. But the tests got done, that's what matters. And it told us what we needed to know to help Pippa,' Ruth said, but Rico was certain she was glossing over much of the struggle she had faced. He wanted to know who had put obstacles in her way. And why. But he let it go...for now.

'The consultant immunologist will test Pippa's antibody levels. The vaccine tests can take up to six weeks, which I know is frustrating, but it is important to define the degree of immunodeficiency,' he explained, seeing the sharp intelligence in Ruth's eyes and knowing she was absorbing all the information. 'If the final diagnosis is CVID—as we believe it will be—Pippa will have immunoglobin replacement therapy, which should help end the cycle of recurring infections.'

'I read that the immunoglobin infusions can be delivered either intravenously or subcutaneously?' Ruth commented, a query in her voice.

Rico nodded, unsurprised by her thoroughness. 'That is so. At first Pippa will have regular treatment at the hospital, but once she is stabilised, and if both mother and daughter can cope, they can be taught how to administer the subcut treatment at home.'

'The subcut sounds scary,' Ruth pointed out. 'Especially for an eight-year-old.'

'Patients generally find it easier than they first think and it is well tolerated. It is better than pro-longed IV access, which can increase the risk of infection and also becomes difficult if the veins are hard to find. And, because the home infu-sions are given once a week, they help to keep the levels more constant than with the IV infusion in hospital,' he reassured her, although her desire to keep her patient informed was typical of the caring doctor he was coming to know.

Aware that time was running out, he ran through some advice and suggestions that Ruth could pass on and which might help the Warrens as they faced the next stage of the journey in gaining a diagnosis and an ongoing treatment programme for Pippa.

A high-voltage smile hit him full on, testing his restraint. 'I'm very grateful, Rico. You've given so much of your time and I know how Judith and Pippa really appreciate your advice. As do I,' she added shyly, touching his heart. And he loved the way she said his name, how her refined English voice, melodious but throaty, made it sound.

'It has been my pleasure to help, *carissima*. And I shall be interested to hear how things progress in the weeks and months ahead. You must keep me up to date.'

'Yes, of course. I'll do that,' she promised.

Rico knew that whatever happened between Ruth and himself in the next couple of days, the Warrens' case would keep their link intact and the avenue of communication open. He obviously didn't like the fact that Pippa was ill, but without Ruth being concerned and searching the internet for information, he would never have met her. And even after a very short time in her company, he could not now imagine his life without Ruth in it. He just hoped he didn't mess things up.

Rico wished the moment of intense closeness could go on forever but, much to his regret, the call came to announce the start of the conference's second session that would take them up to lunch.

'As I have told you in our email exchanges, I am genuinely impressed by your skills. You have an innate gift for learning, Ruth, and for caring, for healing.' Aware of people moving around them and returning to their places in the main room, Rico leaned closer and focused on Ruth. 'We have no more time now, and this afternoon I have the workshop.'

'I'm looking forward to it,' she admitted, making him smile.

Private time with Ruth would be scarce, at least until the evening, but he was determined to be alone with her so he could learn all about her and do everything possible to persuade her to come and work with him. And be with him. Once more the line between professional and personal blurred.

'We can continue our discussion later.' He drew in a deep breath, realising how nervous he was, how desperate to get things right and not scare her away. 'Will you have dinner with me tonight, Ruth?'

Time seemed suspended as he waited for her answer. He felt each beat of his heart beneath his ribs, was sure she must hear its anxious pounding. He watched her changing expressions, wondering what more he could do to convince her, nearly groaning aloud as she nibbled at her bottom lip, making him yearn to taste her, kiss her.

'Yes…I will.'

The whispered words brought untold relief and gratitude that this first hurdle had been crossed. But he knew more lay ahead. They could sort out the details of the evening later. Now he had a few short hours in which to plan his campaign to get Ruth to say yes to a whole lot more than dinner.

CHAPTER THREE

FOR the tenth time in as many minutes, Ruth checked her watch. Any moment now, Rico would arrive to escort her to dinner and her anxiety was growing. As was her excitement. Her whole body felt alive with anticipation, her breathing was too fast and too shallow, and her blood was pulsing wildly though her veins. Unable to settle, she paced across the room and paused at the window, scarcely noticing the view out over the shimmering expanse of Morecambe Bay to the western horizon where the sun would soon be setting.

No matter how many times she told herself that the only reason she had accepted the invitation to have dinner with Rico was because of the work-related discussions they were going to have, she knew it was a lie. Just as she could not deceive herself about the extra effort she had made when getting dressed for the evening. She rarely wore dresses, but as well as insisting on swimwear, in the unlikely event she had time to try out the hotel's indoor pool, Gina and Holly had persuaded her to bring her black dress— standard issue in most women's wardrobes—in case of a smart dinner.

As promised, she had sent her two friends text messages to confirm she had arrived OK, but she had not divulged any information about Rico. Both were nurses. Gina McNaught at Strathlochan's multi-purpose drop-in centre and Holly Tait on the children's ward at Strathlochan Hospital. Both had expressed concern about her intention to accept the last-minute invitation to this conference, although Gina had been the most vociferous.

'Being stuck with two hundred stuffy old doctors for a couple of days doesn't sound like fun to me,' Gina had complained in her soft Scottish burr. 'Besides, you probably know more about the immune system and allergies than most of the delegates, even though you've only been learning about the subjects for the last month.'

Ruth hadn't taken umbrage at the implication that she was a swot because she'd known no judgement had been intended. Not from Gina. Aside from the fact that her friend never said a bad word about anyone, there had been obvious affection and admiration in her voice. Far removed from the criticism, resentment and snideness Ruth had become accustomed to all her life…first at home, then at school, following on during her medical training, and now in her first job as a GP.

'You'll be too busy overseeing final preparations for your wedding on Saturday to even notice I'm away,' Ruth had teased in an effort to reassure her friend.

'I'll notice. And I can't get married without you and Holly beside me as my bridesmaids. So make sure you don't let the mysterious specialist you've been emailing persuade you to disappear off to America to work for him.' Genuine worry had laced Gina's tone. 'Remember how much we all love you here.'

Recalling the words now brought a lump to Ruth's throat, just as they had at the time. She wasn't good at emotion and personal involvement. And she had no idea how to deal with affection, especially when directed at her, as she had never experienced it in her life before. Not until she had arrived in Strathlochan a couple of years ago when, much to her surprise and bemusement, she had immediately been taken under the protective wings of Gina and Holly.

Likewise, the warm and generous welcome she had received from many within the local medical community had been equally unforeseen and overwhelming.

Snapping back to the problem at hand, Ruth nibbled her lower lip in indecision, wondering for the umpteenth time whether to change into something else. Turning round, she cast a nervous glance at her reflection in the hotel room's full-length mirror. The hem of the dress brushed her knees, while the sleeves were three-quarter length and the neckline demure. More than respectable. Not at all revealing. Her freshly washed hair had been left loose, and she was wearing flat shoes, dark tights and the bare minimum of make-up. With her watch and her late grandmother's locket on a chain around her neck her only additions, she should have looked stylish but unnoticeable. Not like a maiden schoolmarm, exactly, but far removed from the sensual siren who now gazed back at her. Her eyes looked huge and startled as she studied her alien image, awed and alarmed at the way the fabric hugged her body, subtly hinting at every curve.

This was *not* the effect she had intended. She had no idea what had gone wrong. And she was certainly nothing like the stranger she saw in the mirror. It had been a while since she had last worn the dress but she didn't remember it ever looking this provocative. Had she realised, she never would have packed it, no matter what Gina and Holly had said.

A sudden knock at the door made her jump and warned her that there was no more time for indecision. Or to change her clothes. Pressing her palms to her cheeks, finding them unusually warm, she walked towards the door, wishing now that she was meeting Rico downstairs amongst the other delegates instead of agreeing that he call for her at her room. Sucking in a steadying breath, sure he would hear each rapid beat of her heart, she opened the door, only for all the air to leave her lungs in a rush when she saw him.

Wearing designer jeans, a black crew-neck sweater and a mid-brown leather jacket, Rico looked casual but smart...and devastatingly handsome. He hadn't shaved, so still had the roguish, bad-boy edge she had uncharacteristically found so sexy when she had first seen him. Her gaze clashed with his and the hunger in gold-flecked hazel eyes seared her to her soul. He took his time looking over her from head to toe and back again, his appreciation so blatant that even she, with her total lack of self-confidence, could not fail to grasp that he liked what he saw.

Ruth shivered. Rico looked as if he wanted to forget all about dinner and would rather stay and feast on her instead. The knowledge weakened her knees. And her resolve. An unrecognisable part of her willed her surrender. A wild and wicked side she had never known she possessed had been fighting for freedom ever since she had met Rico. She had never found pleasure with a man, and her failings as a woman had been well and truly drummed into her, so this new and sudden desire was shocking and bewildering. Her attraction to Rico scared her—almost as much as his apparent attraction to her.

'Good evening, Ruth.' Taking her by surprise, his hands settled on her upper arms and drew her closer so he could place a kiss on each cheek. Her skin tingled from the brush of his lips and her hastily indrawn breath was fragranced with his arousing cedar-wood scent. 'You look beautiful.'

She didn't believe his extravagant compliment, but politeness demanded her response. 'Th-thank you.'

'You are ready to go?' he queried, his hands gliding slowly down her arms before releasing her.

'Yes. I'll just get my things.'

Turning away to pick up her bag and room key, Ruth used the few seconds to try and regain some measure of composure. She only had to be near Rico and her body betrayed her. That the phenomenon had been happening all day, from the first moment they had looked at each other, in no way made it easier for her to understand. Why now? Why this man when no other had ever stirred her interest?

Before she could wrestle with the questions any further, Rico stepped into the room, the door slowly swinging to behind him. 'Allow me to help you with your coat,' he said, picking up the garment she had left draped over the back of a chair.

Ruth frowned in puzzlement. Why did she need to wear a coat to go to dinner in the hotel restaurant? Too on edge to argue, she did as she was bid as he held it ready for her to put on. His solicitousness came as no surprise. She had discovered many times during the day that his manners and courtesy were instinctive, and shown to men, as well as women, young and old alike.

Far too aware of his nearness, Ruth slipped each arm in turn into the coat sleeves, an aching knot forming deep inside her as his hands lingered a moment before gently gathering up the long strands of her hair and easing them out from under the collar, his fingers brushing tantalisingly across the back of her neck. The temptation to remain in his arms, to lean back against him, was hard to resist. Forcing herself to move, she stepped forward, but failed to break the contact between them, or the electric connection, as Rico slowly turned her to face him. Several seconds ticked by as they watched each other in silence.

'Green.'

Ruth stared at him in confusion. 'Excuse me?'

'Your eyes,' he explained, voice husky. 'I expected them to be blue.'

'I'm sorry to disappoint you.'

Her response was sharper than she had intended but his comment had played on her insecurities, her belief that she never met expectations. She turned her head away, discomfited by his inspection, angry with herself for her naivety. Even if she wanted more than the possibility of working with him—which she didn't, she was swift to try and convince herself—she could never be enough for a man as successful, intelligent and good looking as him. The intense and shocking moment of connection when they had first looked at each other had clearly short-circuited her brain.

Ruth was startled when he caught her face, his hold gentle but insistent as he drew her gaze back to his. She couldn't decipher the expression in his eyes, but her own widened in surprise, a tremor running through her as the pad of his thumb brushed across the little indentation between her lower lip and her chin. Her skin tingled from his touch. She'd had no idea she was so sensitive there.

'You mistake my meaning, *carissima*. I was in no way making a complaint.' His voice dropped to a rough purr and her insides clenched in response. The intensity with which he looked at her made her feel as if she were the tastiest morsel he had ever seen and he was very, *very* hungry. 'Your eyes are beautiful. There is nothing remotely disappointing about them—or any part of you.' He paused, regarding her for a moment in speculative silence before stroking his fingertips softly across her cheek, leaving little fires burning in his wake. 'That you should think so is something we will have to address later.' After a quick glance at his watch, he released her. 'Now it is time for us to leave.'

Hooking the strap of her bag over one shoulder, she preceded Rico out of the room and locked the door. As she made to move down the corridor towards the main stairs and lifts, Rico caught her hand, a wicked smile on his face as he led her in the opposite direction.

'Rico, where are we going?' she asked, her fingers linking far too naturally and easily with his.

'We are playing truant, *carissima*.'

The staged whisper, followed by a sexy wink, sent a tremor down her spine. 'What do you mean?' she asked as he opened a door that led to the back stairway used only by staff or in case of emergency.

'If we stay here we will have little peace,' he told her, leading the way down and keeping her close. 'I am selfish enough to want you all to myself, so I have arranged for us to have dinner away from the hotel. If we go down the normal way we will be accosted long before we can reach the front door.' On the ground floor, he peeped down the deserted corridor, then pushed open the fire exit and drew her outside with him, making sure the door clicked safely back into place behind them. 'There is a taxi waiting for us. Our escape to carry out our secret mission is more fun, no?'

It was, Ruth admitted, unable to hold back a smile. She caught his arm as he made to step out into the open, and there was a query in his eyes as he turned back to look at her.

'You make for the car, Agent Linardi, and I'll cover you,' she told him in a terrible attempt at an American accent, ruining her efforts by giggling.

Rico's answering chuckle warmed her from the top of her head to the tips of her toes, as did the delighted appreciation in his eyes that she was playing along. 'Good thinking, Agent Baxter. When I give the signal, make a run for it,' he instructed, adopting an even worse accent than hers.

A moment later Rico waved to her and she hurried across to join him. They were both laughing as he opened the rear door of the taxi and bundled her inside. She slid along the backseat, feeling wonderfully light-hearted as he climbed in beside her, then he leaned forward to greet the driver and give him the address of the restaurant. Not for the first time that day she wondered how this man could make her feel cherished one moment and as if her whole ordered existence was threatened the next.

Rico also made her feel valued. When he had

told her how impressed he was with her quick study and her natural abilities, Ruth had been flattered and warmed by his praise. His words had meant more to her than he, or anyone else, would ever know. People saw her as cool, self-confident, even emotionless, but she was none of those things. That image was a façade, a shield she had cultivated in order to function and to hide the doubts and rejections, the disappointments and lack of self-worth that she had experienced for as long as she could remember.

She may not like it, but she recognised that her craving for acceptance, her need to please and to belong, stemmed back to her childhood. And, deep inside, a part of her still yearned for approval, still struggled to be good enough. Her patients were appreciative, her few friends supportive, but it was Rico who had demonstrated the kind of belief in her that she had once longed, forlornly, to receive from her hyper-critical parents.

Rico had accepted her intelligence and had encouraged her to push herself, challenging her over the past month with the questions he had posed in his emails. She had been fascinated and had spent any spare time studying the topics he had raised—much to the despair of Gina and

Holly, who had literally dragged her out with them on several occasions, claiming she would burn out if she didn't have some fun time. What they couldn't understand was that she thrived on learning and stretching her mind. Rico's emails had invigorated her. In person he was so much more.

As the taxi driver engaged Rico in conversation, Ruth leaned back and reviewed the way the day had unfolded after the morning coffee break. It was hard to believe that she had only met this man in person ten hours ago. She still knew little about him, and yet she felt as if she had known him forever.

When the morning session of talks had ended, Rico had rejoined her, staying close and making sure to sit next to her at lunch. He had introduced her to the people at their table, and to many others during the afternoon, especially those whose work he thought would interest her.

Rico's workshop had been incredible, and although he had often singled her out with testing questions, she hadn't felt awkward, and his obvious approval when she had got things right had made her feel good. As he'd walked around the room, talking, questioning, presenting examples, his brief but frequent touches as he passed her—a hand resting on her shoulder or her head—had seemed to be instinctive, unconscious gestures, and always discreet, out of sight of the other people present. They increased her awareness of him but also gave her the novel feeling of being special and cared for. It had been a heady experience and she feared it would be all too easy to lose her head over this man.

He was very protective and whilst he made her feel incredibly safe, she also knew the very real danger he posed. Aside from his stunning looks, his presence and his masculinity, she was drawn to his intelligence and his humour. And his voice had a crazy effect on her. It couldn't just be his accent, Ruth mused. There were two Italian doctors living and working in or around Strathlochan—Gina's fiancé, who worked with her at the drop-in centre, and Nic di Angelis, a GP from the practice in Lochanrig, one of the neighbouring villages. Both were handsome and charming men, and Ruth was comfortable with them, but neither affected her in the slightest. Not that way. No man ever had. Except Rico.

Ruth was roused from her reverie when the man in question rested one hand on her knee. The touch was light and yet it burned her like a brand, sparking a fresh wave of desire, flames of it flaring through her whole body. The magnetic pull was too strong to resist and she looked at him, feeling the now-familiar jolt as their gazes connected. A slow smile curved his mouth, tightening the ache deep inside her.

'You are all right, *carissima*?'

Ruth wasn't at all sure she was, but she managed a shaky smile in return. 'I'm fine.'

'We are here,' Rico told her, and she realised she had been so engrossed in her thoughts that she had not noticed that the taxi had stopped.

Rico opened the door and climbed out, taking her hand again when she joined him on the pavement. Having thanked and paid the taxi driver, they walked a few yards along the sea-front, enjoying the early evening sun glinting off the expanse of the bay.

'Were we followed, Agent Linardi?' she murmured, pretending to look around and continuing their charade.

A sexy smile curved Rico's mouth. 'I think we have given them the slip for now, Agent Baxter. We can discuss our secret mission while we eat.'

Inside, the restaurant was inviting and warm, with muted lighting, soft background music and a welcoming ambiance. Ruth appreciated Rico's innate good manners as he helped her off with her coat before removing his jacket. He rested a hand on her hip, keeping her close to him. So close she felt his body heat and was aware of and aroused by his heady, masculine scent.

'One of the hotel staff recommended this place,' Rico told her when they had been shown to an alarmingly intimate and secluded table in a quiet corner at the back of the restaurant.

Ruth manufactured a scandalised expression. 'You compromised our mission?'

'Do not worry.' Rico leaned closer, his voice dropping. 'My informant will not give us away.'

The return of the waiter with menus and a basket of bread sticks curtailed further silliness, and Ruth sat back to assess the selection of dishes available.

'If the food is not to your taste, we can go somewhere else,' Rico offered, reverting to his normal voice.

Ruth shook her head. 'No, this is lovely,' she assured him, her mouth watering as she made her choice from the menu.

She liked the fact that Rico asked her opinion. Even when she had asked him not to, Adam had always arrogantly ordered for them both when they had gone out, and she had hated that. Not only had she been perfectly able to make decisions for herself, but he had invariably picked things she did not enjoy and had then had the effrontery to take umbrage if she had not liked something or had asked to change it. Rico, by contrast, treated her with respect, and as an equal,

They sat at the small, attractively set table, out of sight of the other diners in the restaurant. Rico was at right angles to her and so close that his leg brushed against hers. His hand toyed with her fingers or rested on the back of her chair, touching her shoulder, her neck, stroking her hair, and the attention was flattering but overwhelming, keeping her on a knife-edge.

After discussing the food and wine, and discovering that they had similar tastes, they gave their orders to the waiter. Ruth felt relaxed and able to talk to Rico about anything. And he made her laugh as no other man had done. He showed no sign that he found her brains intimidating, something she had encountered so often in the past. It was a refreshing experience and eased some of her tension. Not that she could ever forget or escape the awareness that increased each minute she spent with him. The sexual desire was unfamiliar, scary, yet undeniably exciting. She was completely out of her depth and the only life raft she could cling to was Rico himself—the very cause of her venturing into uncharted waters in the first place.

CHAPTER FOUR

'SO, ARE you a want-to-be female James Bond?' Rico asked when their starters arrived, delighted by the way Ruth had revealed her sense of fun and had played along, turning their escape from the hotel into a game.

Savouring her brown shrimps—which she had told him were a Morecambe Bay speciality—served with hot, buttered, granary toast, Ruth smiled, lighting up their secluded corner of the restaurant. 'Not really. I'm more a closet Miss Marple.'

'Really?' She never ceased to surprise him. 'You like whodunits?'

'I love crime fiction in general. There are many excellent modern writers, but some of my favourites are the older ones like the Father Brown books by G. K. Chesterton and pretty much everything by Agatha Christie,' she elaborated, her enthusiasm evident by the sparkle in her eyes and the tone of her voice. 'Poirot is great, but it was always Miss Marple who appealed to me the most.'

'I bet you have identified the culprit long before the end,' he teased, smiling as a tinge of colour warmed her cheeks and confirmed his suspicion.

'Sometimes.'

Her admission made him chuckle. 'It's that amazing mind of yours. And perfect for immunology which, as I told you earlier, often involves detective work. You are a natural,' he added, appreciating her smile, her quick wit… everything about her.

'How about you?' she asked. 'Did you long to be 007?'

'No, not really. I wanted to be Dirk Pitt,' he confided, naming the well-known lead character from his favourite series of adventure books.

The conversation broadened to other genres of book, and then to movies and music. Enjoying every moment in Ruth's company, Rico took a drink of his wine. He'd nearly been driven to his knees when she had opened her hotel-room door and he'd had his first sight of her in her chic black dress. He had wanted nothing more than to kick the door shut behind him, sweep her into his arms and make love to her all night. She was the most beautiful, sensual, incredible woman he had ever met. And she didn't know it. She had no idea of her power over him, no clue that he was putty in her hands.

Her starter finished, Ruth lightly dabbed rosy lips with her napkin, and his gaze focused on her irresistible mouth. His gut tightened and a fresh wave of desire crashed over him. He longed to taste the sweetness of her and to feel the softness of those lips against his. Meeting her gaze, aware that his hunger for her must be showing in his eyes, he watched the veil of shyness and confusion slide down between them as the fun, sparkly Ruth retreated.

There were so many layers to her personality. Yes, she was beautiful to look at, but it was so much more than her looks that attracted him. He adored everything about her. Her intelligence and quick mind challenged him, her beauty made him weak, her compassion moved him, her skills as a caring doctor impressed him, while her humour and laughter warmed his heart.

He could talk to Ruth about anything. As he already knew from their emails, she was knowledgeable and had her own opinions on things, but she was also open-minded, prepared to consider an issue from another point of view, unafraid to admit it if she subsequently felt she was wrong. Meeting her in person had revealed that they shared many tastes in everyday things but also had similar values on matters of wider and deeper importance.

As their starter plates were cleared away and their main courses set in front of them, he could not stop looking at Ruth. Her eyes captivated him. Framed by long, dusky lashes, they were a bewitching sage green with a narrow dark outer ring around the irises. He wanted to know why his comment about their colour had drawn such a surprising reaction from her…as if he had been criticising, finding fault, proclaiming her less in some way. Nothing could be further from the truth. But the flash of hurt had been genuine and was one of several hints he had gleaned, both from her emails and in the first hours since meeting her, that she had remarkably little confidence in herself as a woman.

Suspicion grew that someone at some time had taken a sledgehammer to her self-esteem and as a result she hid behind her work. She was a superb doctor and he guessed she felt safe and assured in that role, but take that façade away and her confidence ebbed. He wanted to know who had done that to her…and when. And then he wanted to cut away the invisible bonds that held her back from all she could be and watch her bloom and grow and live life to the full. With him.

In the last few years, work had taken precedence in his life. He'd had fun in his youth and as a medical student, knowing full well that most of the women who'd come on to him were interested more in the Linardi name and family money than they were in him as a person. It hadn't mattered because he had always kept everything light-hearted. Unlike his cousin Seb Adriani, he'd never been burned and hurt by a woman. And he had made sure that he never left any broken hearts behind him, either. But he had never lived with a woman, or been involved in a serious relationship and, in his thirty-four years, he had never met a woman who had made him want to embark on one.

Until now. Until Ruth…who had tilted his world on its axis and changed his life.

Both his father and Seb—who was more a brother to him than a cousin—talked of how they had known the moment they had met the right woman. It was something Rico teased them about but which he respected and envied, knowing that it had never happened to him. Today that thunderbolt of knowledge and desire had hit him full on when he had seen Ruth. Now, for the first time, Rico believed that he, too, could know that loving togetherness.

The food was excellent, but Rico was too wrapped up in Ruth to give much thought to his meal. 'What other hobbies and interests do you have away from work?' he asked, eager to know every little detail about her.

'I don't have a lot of free time,' she admitted, nearly giving him heart failure as her tongue-tip peeped out to wipe a spot of sauce from her lower lip. *Dio!* He tried to clear the sudden restriction in his throat and struggled to concentrate on what she was saying. Not easy given the rush of desire and his body's inevitable response. 'I volunteer a few hours each month at a local clinic for homeless people and others, such as migrants, who are without access to regular health care. And, when my hours allow, I volunteer at the animal rescue centre.'

Doing things for others rather than herself, Rico noted, not at all surprised. 'What about time just for you?'

'My friends and I go out to the cinema or for a meal, and we'll often have a girls' night in, relaxing with a bottle of wine, all talking at once, and eating far too much chocolate,' she added with a bewitching chuckle. 'I'm not very sporty, but I like to swim…and go for long walks. Most of all, I enjoy learning new things.'

'Do you have pets of your own?' Rico asked, captivated by her, and barely tasting his meal of fresh local fish.

'No. Although I've always wanted to.' She took a sip of her wine, then set down her glass, her slender fingers toying with the stem. 'I was never allowed pets when I was young, I…'

Rico watched her, silently urging her to continue, sensing a moment of inner turmoil as a shadow clouded her eyes. Her words concerned him and made him wonder about her childhood. Had it not been a happy one? Before he could find a way to ask that would not have her retreating from him even further, she gave an imperceptible shake of her head and the moment was gone.

'With the hours I work, it isn't practical at the moment, but hopefully that will change one day. Until then I get to babysit my friends' animals when they are away, and enjoy the ones at the rescue centre. I sometimes wonder if maybe I should have been a vet.'

There was humour in her words but also the edge of something else. Something dark and sad. There was so much more to learn about her and her life, and they had not yet begun to talk about work and whether she would be interested in a change of direction in her career. He had asked her to come here because he had wanted to offer her a job…having met her, he wanted so much more.

The time was ticking by far too quickly and he was becoming more resentful of the conference's demands, greedier for her company, and hungrier to have her in his arms. If he didn't touch her soon, he'd go crazy. And before too much longer, he *had* to kiss her. He hoped the time would come when he could touch her freely, could hold her, and make love to her.

Her meal finished, Ruth sat back and tucked a strand of pale gold hair behind her ear. His fingers tingled, remembering the feel of her hair when he had helped her on with her coat. The strands had been even silkier than he had anticipated. And her skin even softer. He had not been able to resist lingering, leaning close to breathe in her scent—lavender and her own unique womanly fragrance. Essence of Ruth. It had taken every ounce of willpower to release her, to not pull her into his arms and kiss her as he so yearned to do.

'I'm sorry.'

Ruth's words startled him from his reverie. 'Sorry? Whatever for?'

'I must have bored you, talking so much about myself,' she explained, revealing once more the insecurities of the woman who shielded herself behind her work.

Taking one of her hands, smaller and more delicate than his, he held it between his palms, exploring the shape of her fingers, learning the feel of her, amazed at the softness of her skin and the contrast of her pale colouring against his darker tones. Even this simple touch caused his heart rate to kick up.

'What nonsense! You could never, ever bore me, Ruth,' he reassured her, determined to set her misconceptions to rest and to make her understand how much he valued her, personally and professionally. He met her gaze, seeing a whole mix of emotions vying for supremacy in those gorgeous green eyes. 'I want to know all there is to know about you.'

Cradling her hand, he stroked her fingers and traced circles on her palm with the pad of his thumb. The zing of electricity crackled between them like a living thing. His fingers picked up the rapid beat of the pulse in her wrist and he knew she was as affected as he was. He drew her hand towards him and placed a kiss to her palm, feeling the tremor that rippled through her.

The evening was marching on and there was much more he needed to know if he hoped to succeed in winning Ruth in every way. Not wanting to make her uncomfortable by pushing too much on the personal details about her, he turned his attention to her current job. He frowned, remembering something from their conversation that morning that he had filed away to explore when they were alone.

'Tell me more about your job, *carissima*, and what happened when Judith first brought Pippa to see you. You said earlier that there had been a query over you requesting the blood tests.'

Whilst every cell in her body was conscious of Rico and the sensation of his touch, her hand in his, his lips brushing softly across her palm, she was thankful that the conversation had returned to more comfortable ground. She rarely talked about herself, even to Gina and Holly, the only real friends she'd ever had, so the fact that she had been so open with Rico amazed her. Why she should be so surprised, she didn't know. She had been acting completely out of character ever since she had first set eyes on him that morning, and the awareness, desire and electrically charged connection were increasing, not diminishing.

Trying to ignore the tingling sensation as his fingers caressed hers, Ruth focused on what he had asked her and briefly recapped on the information about the Warrens she had given in her emails. Warning bells had begun ringing as soon as Judith Warren and her eight-year-old daughter, Pippa, had stepped into her consulting room back in April and, after listening to the extensive and complicated history, and then examining Pippa, it had been obvious that something serious was going on.

Rico's help and advice had led her to the possible diagnosis of CVID. A disorder of the immune system, CVID resulted in a deficiency of serum immunoglobin, meaning low levels of antibodies and an increased susceptibility to infections that the body was unable to fight off.

'I forgot to tell you this morning that I've put Judith and Pippa in touch with the Primary Immunodeficiency Association,' she told him. 'They're finding a lot of support on the forum, and Judith said it was especially useful being able to talk with other patients who have immunodeficiency diseases, and to parents who have children with CVID.'

'I am glad. But I feel sure that the support the Warrens are most grateful for has been your own. They know how blessed they are to have found you.'

Rico's continued approval and belief in her brought a warm glow. No one had ever given her the kind of backing he did and she had no idea how to deal with it. Feeling awkward, she looked down at the table, her hair falling forward to mask her expression. A second later Rico's fingers were gently tucking her hair back behind her ear.

'Why is it so difficult for you to accept your own worth, *carissima*?' he asked, the soft huskiness of his accented voice and the sure touch of his hand cradling hers making her pulse race and her nerve-endings jump. 'Is it so unusual for people to praise you and show appreciation for your skills and understanding and your caring heart?'

'Rico…' She broke off, unsure what to say, relieved when the waiter arrived to remove their empty plates and take the order for their desserts, as it gave her a moment to try and gather her scattered thoughts.

'Talk to me, Ruth.'

How had Rico ended up even closer to her? His leg pressed against hers and one arm rested along the back of her chair, his hand toying with her hair. 'I enjoy helping my patients…and they're grateful.' She felt ridiculously out of breath. Her voice sounded uneven, as much from the effect of his touch than her discomfort at his questions.

'I am not surprised. You are an incredible doctor. But what of your colleagues? And your boss?' His fingers slid beneath her hair, the tips of them tracing devastating circles on the back of her neck, making it impossible for her to concentrate. 'Were they not happy that you diagnosed Pippa and proud of what you had achieved?'

'The senior partner backed me,' she told him, trying to sound positive and conceal both her disappointment with the problems at work and her response to his caressing fingers.

'As he should have done. They all should have supported you,' Rico insisted, his annoyance on her behalf clear. 'Why did they not?'

'Things were difficult.'

'Difficult how?'

Ruth hesitated, but her defences were already lowered by Rico's faith in her and by her body's continued surrender to his closeness, his touch, his subtle scent, and she found herself confiding in him. 'Graeme Campbell, a junior partner in the practice, was one of the doctors who had previously seen Pippa. The Warrens joined our practice last Christmas and saw Graeme several times in the next few months as Pippa had a couple of severe chest infections, breathing problems and other issues. Graeme's attitude was the same as the doctors they had seen in the past. Then someone recommended that Judith bring Pippa to me. Graeme didn't like it—especially when my diagnosis proved to be right.'

She felt Rico tense, and his fingers stilled their soft, erotic caresses, sliding round to cup her face and bring her gaze to his. 'You mean this man resented that you had done your job properly, had taken the time and made the effort to see beneath the surface and had not given up or taken the easy route by dismissing the Warrens…as he had done?'

'Something like that.' Given how protective Rico had been of her all day, she shouldn't be surprised by the fire in his eyes, but it was such a novel experience and took some getting use to. 'Graeme felt I had shown him up and questioned his skills.'

Rico shook his head. 'He has no one to blame but himself, *carissima*. He failed to listen to Judith or to take account of Pippa's medical history.'

'I know. But it made the situation…awkward. Especially as there was already tension between

Graeme and myself. We got off to a rocky start from the day I began working there two years ago,' she admitted, wondering if she could have done anything differently.

'He made you unwelcome?'

Ruth released a heavy sigh as she thought back to her first day at work in Strathlochan. She had been nervous, anxious to please, wanting so badly to be accepted by the staff there. Most had been friendly, but one or two had been standoffish, including a couple of the younger doctors who had followed Graeme Campbell's lead, and Janet Dalrymple, one of the receptionists, who made no secret of her affection for Graeme.

'My first day at the surgery coincided with one of the regular meetings, when the doctors, practice and district nurses, and other support staff get together to discuss cases, raise any issues or ask for advice,' she explained, pausing as the waiter set down the desserts which both she and Rico ignored.

'Go on,' he encouraged, the hand holding hers giving a gentle squeeze.

'During the meeting, mention was made of a patient whose symptoms were puzzling everyone. I looked over the notes and listened to what the doctors and the district nurses were saying, and it sounded familiar, mirroring a case I had seen during my GP training year.'

Rico smiled and she was momentarily struck dumb by his effect on her and by the expression that gleamed in his eyes. 'And you were able to give a diagnosis,' he said, more statement of fact than query.

'Yes.'

'That's my Ruth.' He raised her hand so he could place another brief but tantalising kiss on her palm. 'I am sorry. I interrupted you. Please, continue.'

It took a moment for Ruth to regain her composure, and not just from his intimate touch, his belief in her or the way he was now caressing her fingers. It was what he had said. *His* Ruth? It was the second time today he had said that and the possessive pride shocked her, warmed her, scared her.

'Ruth?' he pressed.

'OK.' She took a steadying breath and tried to focus on what she had been saying. 'I did make a suggestion to them…bollus pemphigoid,' she told him, noting his surprised reaction. 'It turned out that I was right.'

'But, of course.'

He sounded so adamant, so free of doubt, that she couldn't help but smile, amazed at his acceptance of her. 'David Robson—he's the senior partner, along with his wife, Catriona, who is also a doctor there—said it wasn't a condition he had seen in all his years as a GP, and he was impressed and grateful that I had.'

'But others didn't share his view?'

'Not all of them,' she admitted. 'Graeme Campbell was displeased. Away from the meeting he tried to make out that I was showing off, saying that I thought I was better than the rest of them and trying to suck up to David because I was new there.' She broke off a moment, remembering how she had felt, the sinking feeling that here was someone else who resented her love of learning and her curious mind—who couldn't accept women doctors as their equal. 'It wasn't like that at all.'

Rico's fingers linked with hers. 'I know, *carissima*. Your only thought was to help the patient.'

'Yes.'

Again Rico understood her. Things had been difficult with Graeme from that moment. He did as little work as possible and was more inter-ested in golf and womanising than he was in his career. It hadn't helped things between them when he had made inappropriate comments and tried several times to come on to her. She had turned him down. He hadn't liked the rejection. And he had made life difficult for her at work, souring the atmosphere, and turning his friends on the staff against her. Ruth refrained from mentioning any of that to Rico, however, returning instead to the Warren case.

'When I mentioned Pippa and CVID, Graeme was angry and urged caution, but David, Catriona and the other senior doctors were prepared to back me and trust my instincts,' she explained, leaving out the unpleasantness that had ensued and Graeme's nasty tirade when he had got her on her own.

'And this attitude is not unusual for you? It has happened often?' Rico queried with a frown.

Ruth gave a careless shrug. 'If you have brains, and you use them, some people resent it or think you are competing or showing off, especially if you are a woman,' she told him, although her attempt to be blasé and pretend it didn't matter failed.

'Which shows only how shallow and sad and stupid those people are.' Rico was silent for a moment, absently playing with her fingers. Then he looked up and a tremor rippled through her at the fire of determination and the blatant sensual hunger in his gold-speckled hazel eyes.

'Ruth, there is something we have yet to discuss. Already I feel I have known you for ever. One day is nearly over and there is so much more I want to ask and to learn about you. But hearing you speak like this, sensing there is a part of you that is not happy or fulfilled or appreciated, makes me rush ahead.'

Her pulse began racing, and she couldn't pull enough breath into her lungs as she waited for Rico to continue, frightened that she knew what he was going to say, even more scared that she would be swept along by the special and potent connection between them and agree to something with her heart rather than her head. Rico drew her hand towards him until her palm was resting against his chest, pressed there by his own. Beneath the expensive wool of his jumper she could feel the rapid beat of his heart.

'Rico…' Her whispered protest was silenced as he placed a finger on her lips.

'I know it is too soon, *carissima*, but—'

Whatever he had been about to say was cut off by a fearful bang and crash from the kitchen, followed at once by a heart-wrenching scream and several other voices raised in alarm. Rico released her hand and they both rose instinctively, rushing out of their secluded alcove and into the main part of the restaurant. The kitchen door burst open, increasing the volume of the commotion within. Face white with shock, the manager looked at the startled diners frozen in place at their tables.

'There's been an accident,' he explained, his voice wavering. 'Is there anyone here who knows first aid?'

All else forgotten in the urgency of the moment, Ruth stepped forward, knowing Rico was beside her. 'We're doctors,' she told the shaken manager. 'What's happened? What can we do?'

CHAPTER FIVE

As THE door of the hospital waiting room opened, Rico glanced up from the magazine he was idly flicking through, but it was a nurse who came in and not Ruth.

'Dr Linardi, the car is here to take you and Dr Baxter home,' the young woman informed him.

'Thank you.' Tossing the magazine back on the table, he rose to his feet and stretched weary limbs before crossing the room. He was eager to meet up with Ruth who had set off in search of the ladies' cloakroom some while ago and had yet to return. 'And Dr Baxter—do you know where she is?'

Nodding, the nurse gestured down the corridor towards the A and E department. 'The young man's parents asked to speak to her. They would like a quick word with you, too, before you go. I'll show you the way.'

As Rico followed the nurse he thought back over the last couple of hours. The evening had certainly not gone the way he had hoped, although the unfortunate accident at the restaurant had prevented him from making a huge mistake and rushing Ruth too quickly with his appeal for her to come and work with him. Having her by his side—at work and at home— was what he wanted, more now than ever. And after listening to her, reading between the lines at all she had left unsaid, he was sure she was not happy and fulfilled in her current job.

He was glad that her boss was supportive of her. Clearly the man could see how dedicated and genuine Ruth was, and recognised her superb skills and intelligence. But that did not apply to all her colleagues and Rico felt a cold knot of anger form inside him as he thought of the selfish young GP who had made life difficult and unpleasant for Ruth. He suspected there was much that Ruth had not told him about Graeme Campbell, but even after one day, he knew her well enough to pick up on her discomfort when she had mentioned the man.

He had also sensed Ruth's deep-seated aloneness, the layers of suppressed emotion, and her struggle for acceptance, things he felt sure stretched back into her past rather than relating solely to her present post. That knowledge, and the desire for her not to be alone any more, had driven him to so nearly make his offer of a job. That Ruth loved the day-to-day work with patients was obvious, but her workplace did not provide the support and the challenges she needed. He was sure of it. Now he had to find a better time and a better way to discuss the future.

The nurse halted outside a small room and knocked on the closed door, opening it and saying a few words before moving back to allow him to enter. Rico thanked her and went in, his gaze immediately settling on Ruth. She looked up, green eyes cloudy with fatigue, her welcoming smile tired but enough to send a jolt to his heart. He sat down next to her, automatically reaching for her hand and giving it an understanding squeeze before he turned his attention to the anxious couple opposite.

'Mr and Mrs Michaels, this is Dr Linardi,' Ruth introduced. 'He was at the restaurant, too, and did much to help when Jamie was injured.'

'I did nothing more than support Ruth. The skill was all hers,' Rico insisted, but Jamie's parents would hear no argument and were effusive in their thanks.

'We don't know what would have happened had the pair of you not been there and acted so quickly,' Mr Michaels said.

Mrs Michaels nodded tearfully, shredding a damp paper tissue in her hands. 'We're so grateful to you both. The consultant here says that Jamie's condition would be much worse without your quick action and care of him. They plan to transfer him to a specialist burns unit,' she explained, fresh tears welling.

'That's where Jamie will get the very best care, treatment and rehabilitation,' Ruth explained gently.

As she tried to reassure the couple, Rico returned the grip of her fingers, offering his silent support. He knew that Jamie had a long recovery ahead of him after the freak accident that had seen his hands, arms, neck, shoulders and chest suffer serious burns. He had slipped on some spilled oil that had not been properly cleaned away, and he had instinctively reached out to try to save himself, landing on the working gas rings and setting fire to some of his clothing. Thrashing around in fear, momentum had seen him fall to the floor, unfortunately dragging two large pans of boiling water down on top of him. The flames had been extinguished but they had already done some damage, only increased by the scalding water.

Ruth had taken charge in the chaotic kitchen,

instructing someone to call an ambulance while she set about caring for twenty-year-old Jamie, the terrified trainee chef, removing any items of clothing and accessories that were not adhered to his skin. After soothing and cooling the burns with water, Ruth had then had started to cover some of the injured areas with cling film, careful not to wrap it around Jamie's limbs so that if they began to swell, they would not be constricted. The cling film protected against infection, shielded the burned flesh from the air and so helped reduce the pain, yet still allowed the injured areas to be seen.

The paramedics had swiftly joined them, and had been impressed by Ruth's treatment and quick thinking. Her knowledge and competence had been no surprise to Rico, however. Once IV access had been gained and pain relief given, Jamie had been gently lifted onto a stretcher and taken out of the restaurant. There had been no hesitation when the paramedics had asked for Ruth to accompany them in the ambulance, and Jamie, unsurprisingly, had not wanted to let go of her hand. Having refused point blank to abandon Ruth, Rico had grabbed her bag and his jacket, and had gone along, too.

Given the extent of Jamie's injuries, the ambulance had bypassed the local hospital, whose casualty services had been scaled down, and had rushed him to the nearest city hospital with full accident and emergency facilities. Once there, Rico had joined Ruth in giving the trauma team a detailed debrief of all that had happened before and after the arrival of the paramedics.

'The car is waiting for us,' he told Ruth now, concerned for her and eager to get her back to the hotel for some rest.

Much to his relief, Ruth nodded her agreement and rose to her feet, almost swaying with exhaustion. He slipped his arm round her, tucking her close to his side, his hand cupped possessively over the curve of her hip. They said goodbye to Mr and Mrs Michaels—who had Ruth's email address so they could send updates on Jamie's progress—and left the shaken parents in the care of a nurse who would escort them back to their son.

'I hope Jamie will be all right,' Ruth murmured as they walked towards the main exit, outside where the car waited to take them back to the hotel.

'He has the best chance thanks to you.' Rico shook his head, proud of the calm efficiency and compassion she had displayed while aiding Jamie. 'You were amazing, *carissima*.'

Aware that Ruth's coat had been left at the restaurant in the confusion, Rico took off his leather jacket and slipped it around her shoulders, his blood heating at the way she snuggled into it, closing her eyes for a moment as if savouring his warmth and his scent.

Ruth's sweet smile stole his breath. 'I couldn't have done it without your help.'

'Nonsense,' he chided softly as they climbed into the back of the car.

As she stifled a yawn, he drew her into his arms where she nestled, unresisting. There was so much more he wanted to say, and so much he still had to learn about her, but it was very late and she was visibly weary. Which was inevitable as she came down from the charge of adrenalin she had been running on since the accident. To prove his point, within seconds she was asleep. Smiling, he cradled her close, the fingers of one hand softly stroking the fall of her silky hair as he relished the feel of her against him.

Her lavender scent teased him. It was an old-fashioned fragrance, one he usually associated with his grandmother. Nonna Emanuela was eighty years old and a real character. Yet on Ruth the lavender's subtle freshness was innocent yet heady. Wholesome. And mixed with her own unique womanliness it was sensual and arousing. Everything about her was surprising and unexpected. He felt dizzy and off balance with the way she had changed his whole world since the moment he had first set eyes on her. It was hard to believe that was less than twenty-four hours ago.

Some while later, Rico looked out of the window into the darkness of the night as the car skimmed the edge of Morecambe Bay. The waters gleamed black and mysterious under the crescent moon that hung high in the clear, inky, star-dusted sky. Then the driver turned between the stone gateposts that marked the entrance to the hotel, and pulled up in front of the imposing building, bringing their journey, and his opportunity to hold Ruth in his arms, to an end.

'Ruth?'

Rico hated to wake her, hated even more that he would have to let her go. He gently stroked one downy-soft cheek, the reflection of light spilling out from the hotel casting the shadows of her long sooty eyelashes on her skin. His lips brushed across her forehead.

'We are here, *carissima*,' he told her, running one hand up and down her arm, giving her a gentle shake. 'Come on, sleeping beauty, it is time to wake up.'

'Hmm...?'

An endearing frown knotted her brow as she stirred, firing his blood as she stretched sinuously against him. Her eyes slowly opened and focused sleepily on his, a becoming blush pinkening her cheeks as she realised just how close they were. Her movements were jerky and uncoordinated as she drew away. Rico reluctantly released her, allowing her to put some distance between them.

'I'm sorry, I must have fallen asleep,' she murmured, her voice unsteady, her hands fussing with her hair before smoothing down the skirt of her dress.

'There is nothing to apologise for.' Far from it. The fifteen minutes he had been able to cuddle her close had been heavenly...but all too short. 'It has been a busy day, not helped by the events of the evening.'

After thanking the driver and discovering he had already been paid, Rico climbed out and waited for Ruth. A moment of hesitation followed, then she accepted the hand he held out to her, her palm sliding across his before their fingers entwined, hers looking pale and delicate against his darker ones. He adjusted his jacket around her shoulders as they walked towards the entrance in the chill of the night air. The door, locked at this hour, was opened for them by a concerned night porter called Charlie, who informed them that the news of what had happened at the restaurant had filtered through. Indeed, the restaurant manager had located Ruth's coat and returned it to the hotel, offering his thanks for their help, refusing payment for their unfinished meal, and inviting them back any time for dinner on the house.

Taking their leave of Charlie, they head towards the stairs. Ruth slipped off his jacket and handed it back, tossing her coat over one forearm. Not wanting to be parted from her, Rico escorted her to her room, sensing the growing tension in the silence, and the shimmering electricity that always sparked when they were together.

'The evening didn't go quite how I expected,' he said when they reached her door.

'I know.' Ruth's smile was wry. 'But I enjoyed it, thank you. The meal was lovely. And I learned a lot to share with Judith and Pippa.'

He took her free hand in both of his, craving the physical contact. 'There is still much for us to discuss. But that can wait until tomorrow—or later today,' he corrected with a rueful smile after a glance at his watch. 'I liked being with you this evening, *carissima*,' he told her, tucking a strand of hair back behind her ear, his fingers lingering, caressing her baby-soft skin.

'Rico…'

Uncertainty wavered in her voice. He looked into stunning eyes, seeing the dawning awareness in their depths before his gaze dropped to her mouth. The temptation was too much. He could not resist another second.

'I have to kiss you.' Her eyes widened in response to his husky, needy appeal, and he felt the tremor that ran through her. Conscious of her wariness, and determined to build the trust between them, he tried to rein in his urgent hunger and asked her to make the decision— praying she would agree. 'May I, Ruth?'

Rico held his breath as the seconds ticked by and he waited for her answer. Anxiety, longing, doubt, excitement, even a flash of fear showed in her rapidly changing expressions. He wanted to unravel all those emotions, to understand what lay behind them, but further questions would have to wait until later because Ruth nodded her assent and drove every thought from his brain.

Knowing her nervousness, he endeavoured to

keep his desire in check. He cupped her face, his heart pounding and his chest tight, feeling as awkward as a callow youth about to experience his first kiss. He'd never been so jittery, but this moment was one of the most important of his life as it *was* his first kiss with Ruth. And it was vital that he do this right.

He called on every scrap of patience he possessed and took his time, determined not to rush her. First he kissed her forehead, then the tip of her nose. He kissed each closed eyelid in turn before whispering kisses down one cheek and around the curve of her jaw. Ruth swayed towards him, her hands inching up to his shoulders, fingers tightening as he teased a kiss to the corner of her mouth and lightly nibbled his way across the swell of her lower lip to the other corner. Rico's gut knotted as she moaned, instinctively turning her head as her mouth sought his. Unable to wait another moment, he set his lips to hers, tentatively at first, learning, exploring, savouring this special moment.

Any plan he had to take this slowly, to be gentle, even chaste, evaporated in the first second. The instant their mouths met, the passion bubbling just beneath the surface ignited, and he could no more halt the onrushing need than he could stop breathing. The craving to taste her was irresistible. He whispered the tip of his tongue along the seam of her luscious lips and they parted in instant invitation. An invitation he needed no prompting to accept.

It was as if a match had been set to a tinderbox, setting off an unprecedented explosion of hungry passion that consumed everything... every part of them fusing together. One taste, he had told himself. But he knew from the first that one taste of Ruth was never going to be enough. She was like nectar. An elixir. Addictive, potent and heavenly. Patience snapping, he slid one hand back to fist in the silken strands of her hair, while the other grazed down her spine to the tempting curve of her derrière, urging her against him, needing her as close as possible as the kiss moved from slow exploration to drugging possession.

Ruth's soft whimper of surrender undid him. As did her shy but eager participation as he changed the angle and deepened the kiss even further. She responded instinctively to the hot passion of their kiss, her fingers spearing into his hair and her body arching into him. Her inexperience was obvious. Wonderful, yet hard to understand. But he was so swept away on the rolling tide of desire that nothing else mattered as he learned every contour of her mouth, savoured her sweetness, and encouraged her to explore in return. He teased her tongue, stroking and gliding, sucking on her, drawing her into his mouth.

He had never experienced this runaway urgency before, and he lost all reason, forgetting where they were, forgetting that this was meant to be a gentle first kiss. Groaning, driven to the edge by his need of her, he took more, intensifying the contact, drunk on her taste, her scent, his hips rocking against hers, his body hot and tight with arousal. For a few more endless minutes Ruth was with him, just as demanding, just as involved...and then he sensed the change in her. She started to tense and then to pull back. As her withdrawal registered, Rico struggled to think of her needs and not his own, putting the brakes on, easing them down, gentling and soothing her as the fiery, erotic kiss came to an end.

Rico opened his eyes and focused on Ruth's face. She looked like a doe caught in the headlights. Desire was evident in her green eyes, but it was offset now by confusion, shock and a touch of fright. Her breathing was as ragged as his own and he could see the wild beat of her pulse at the hollow of her throat, one that matched the pounding of his heart.

His fingertips skimmed over her flushed cheeks, the pad of his thumb tracing rosy, kiss-swollen lips. 'It is all right, *carissima.*'

'Rico, I have to go now.' Her words were nearly as shaky as her hands, betraying her nervous state as she fumbled for her key.

'I know,' he reassured her.

And he did know…but it didn't mean he liked it. As she retreated from him, emotionally and physically, he berated himself for allowing things to get so out of hand, for rushing her when he knew she wasn't ready. But the blaze of passion… *Dio!* It was incredible between them. The last thing he wanted to do was to leave her alone, but he knew he must. For now. If he pushed too much he would frighten her away, and already the kiss had raged way beyond what he had intended. The power of what they shared had spooked her. He didn't know why, or what lay behind her inexperience and lack of self-confidence as a woman, but he intended to find out.

'Sleep well, Ruth,' he said now, holding the door open for her but reluctantly remaining on the wrong side of it in the deserted corridor. He hoped she would rest and that the incident with Jamie would not prey on her mind. 'You have my mobile number. Call me any time if you need anything or you want to talk. Promise me.' She nodded, but lashes lowered to hide her expression. He tipped up her chin and waited for her to look at him. 'Goodnight, *carissima*. We will talk again later.'

'Goodnight.'

Slowly he released her and, after a few more silent moments, the charge fizzing between them, she stepped back and closed the door. Rico stood and stared at it, willing for it to open again and for Ruth to change her mind, knowing that she wouldn't. Her air of innocence was real. There were no pretensions about her. He was more and more attracted to her, and more determined than ever that he had to find a way round the complications of the clash of his professional life and his personal life.

He walked to his own room, knowing he would never be able to sleep for thinking about her, wanting her, wishing he was spending the night with her in his arms. He frowned as he thought of those flashes of genuine fright in her eyes and his earlier suspicions grew that someone at some time had hurt her. Badly enough that the heady passion and loss of control scared her. A cold rage combined with the searing ache in his gut. He needed to find out what had happened so that he could help to release the sensual side of her that was so seldom allowed free rein.

A while later, he lay on his bed and stared at the ceiling. He had only a few hours left to come up with a workable plan—one that would persuade Ruth to stay and so buy him some time to earn her trust and to convince her that her future lay with him. In every way.

If she didn't know better, she would think the last twenty-four hours had been a dream, Ruth admitted, reaching the end of the pool and doing a lazy tumble-turn before starting another length.

Despite all the upheaval—perhaps *because* of it—she had only managed a few snatches of sleep. She had woken up shortly before five a.m., and, after tossing and turning for a while, wide-awake, her mind abuzz, she had given in. Putting on her two-piece swimsuit she had wrapped herself in a towelling robe and tiptoed through the hotel. Everywhere had been deserted, the only noises coming from the kitchen, and Ruth had been glad to have the indoor pool to herself.

Aside from her love of learning, swimming was her main hobby and relaxation away from work. Having swum competitively for her school and county in her youth, when living in the south of England, she still swam every day if she could. That Strathlochan had a superb fifty-metre pool—one of many excellent facilities in the town's combined leisure centre—had been one of the reasons she had moved there. She usually found the exercise both invigorating and soothing, but alone in the semi-darkness of the much smaller hotel pool, her thoughts continued to intrude.

Strathlochan made her think of Gina and Holly, both of whom had left text messages on her mobile phone. She had sent noncommittal replies, saying that the conference was interesting and she was being kept busy, but declining to mention anything about Rico. She had no idea what to say about him and, at the moment, it was all too new and confusing to share.

This time yesterday, Rico had still been a stranger with whom she had shared a month-long, work-related email correspondence. One day later and it felt as if her whole life, her very being, had shifted on its axis and she had no idea whether she would ever be able to steer her way back onto her familiar course again. More worrying still was whether she even wanted to. A traitorous, formerly hidden part of her yearned for something different in both her professional and private lives, and recognised that Rico could be the one to deliver those changes. But another part of her, the sensible, cautious Ruth, used to being alone, was too scared to step into the unknown.

She thought of the previous evening, of the awfulness of Jamie's injuries, and of how wonderful Rico had been…not only in his compassion towards the young man but also in his support of her. He had backed her completely, never once trying to take control, and she had been surprised that he had settled so happily into a secondary role. In her experience, most male doctors she had met would have tried to assert themselves. Rico had been a staunch ally, both at the restaurant and at the hospital. His presence, and his belief in her, had made her feel good.

Then there was *the kiss*. A tremor ran through her as the memory, so vivid, replayed itself again and again. It was an unfortunate analogy given what had happened at the restaurant, but the only way to describe the enormity of what had happened when Rico had kissed her was that her whole body had been consumed by heat.

Flames had licked at every part of her, searing her deep inside, firing her blood. It had been too much, yet not enough. She had been over-whelmed, the explosion of passion and urgent need clamouring within her so new and powerful it had frightened her. She had never imagined anything like it before and couldn't comprehend what was happening to her. She was never out of control. And she had never responded like that in her life, had never believed she could, not after everything Adam had said, and certainly not from one kiss.

But *what* a kiss! Ruth groaned, putting in a couple of fast lengths, but nothing dulled the memory, or the unfulfilled desire she still felt, and she stopped swimming, floating on her back as she gazed up at the shadowy reflections on the ceiling. She had to be losing her mind. Shaky fingers touched her lips, finding them still plump and sensitised. And she could still taste Rico…hot, exotic, male, exciting, wicked. Her hands skimmed down her body, over breasts that felt unusually sensitive, to rest low on her abdomen where an unfamiliar aching knot con-tinued to niggle, leaving her edgy and restless.

She was so confused. She didn't want to be attracted to Rico—or to any man. For her, sex was overrated, and Adam had left her in no doubt that she was useless at it. Yet she had exploded like a rocket on Bonfire Night when Rico had kissed her. He only had to look at her, let alone touch her, for her heart to pound and her body to react in unfamiliar ways. She'd never felt anything like it before. And it scared her. Work was her focus. She couldn't allow any distractions.

Even more terrifying was the thought of working for Rico, being around him, keeping work and her crazy attraction to him separate. Nothing had yet been said aloud, but she was certain that he had been about to raise the subject at the restaurant before Jamie's accident had silenced him. Part of her was enthused and excited by the prospect of all he could teach her about immunology. The other part of her, programmed for self-preservation, demanded she run as far and as fast as she could because he was dangerous to her heart, her very being. She had no idea what to do. But she couldn't risk throwing away what might be the most wonderful career opportunity she would ever have by indulging in a one-night stand with her potential boss.

Sighing, she rolled over and completed

another length of butterfly. She turned at the end of the pool, holding onto the side for a moment, a gasp of shock escaping when she looked up and saw Rico watching her from the side of the pool. Dressed in a pair of skimpy black swim trunks that left nothing to the imagination, the masculine perfection of his body took her breath away. Ruth was surprised the water wasn't boiling and steaming given how her temperature flared just looking at him.

Her heart was beating far too fast—and not because of her exercise. She watched, her breath ragged and the aching knot deep inside her tightening unbearably, as Rico executed a perfect dive into the water and demonstrated an expert freestyle as he swam down the length of the pool. Skittish and wary, Ruth pushed off, swimming away from him. But no matter how she tried to keep a safe distance between them, Rico moved inexorably closer, until they both ended up at the shallow end of the pool.

'You are a very graceful and skilful swimmer,' he praised, edging closer.

'Thank you.' She could feel her cheeks warm in response to his words and his approval. 'So are you.'

Rico stood up, sweeping wet, over-long dark

hair back from his handsome, unshaven face, and Ruth leaned back against the tiled wall for support. Ducking low so the water covered her shoulders, she tried to forget how luxuriant and unexpectedly soft his hair had felt last night when her fingers had tunnelled into it. He stepped towards her and her gaze drank in the sight of his athletic body with broad shoulders and lean, strong torso. Water droplets zigzagged down olive-toned skin, over the corded, rippling muscles of his arms and chest. A smattering of dark hair nestled between well-defined pecs, and a narrow line led down from his navel. Her disobedient gaze followed it under the water-line to where it dipped below the low-slung swim trunks, lingering before she was able to force it to climb back up the impressive body to safer territory. Ruth sucked in a breath, clenching her hands to stop herself giving in to the compulsion to reach out and touch him.

Rico apparently had no such hesitation. He sank back into the water in front of her until his gaze was on the same level as hers, the gold-speckled eyes reflecting warmth, concern and an unashamed hunger he made no effort to hide. A hunger that called to her, excited her and alarmed her. He lightly grazed the knuckles of one hand down her cheek, making her skin tingle, then the pad of his thumb brushed over lips that still carried the memory of their erotic kiss.

'Could you not sleep?' he asked her, the husky, accented voice sending a shiver down her spine.

She shook her head, swallowing the restriction in her throat as his fingertips traced the outline of her jaw before fluttering down her throat. 'I did for a while, but once I was awake…' Her words trailed off as the movement of the water carried them closer to each other, their legs tangling together and sending fresh waves of sensation scudding through her.

'Me, too.' He caught her hands in his, his voice dropping to a sexy purr as he drew her inexorably closer. 'What are you doing to me, *sirena mia*?'

'What does that mean?' Her own voice came out on a whisper as she struggled to focus and counteract the sensual brush of the hair-dusted skin of his legs against the smoothness of her own.

'My mermaid,' he told her, the expression in his eyes growing ever hotter. 'You have bewitched me, cast a spell on me—like a siren, luring me to my downfall.'

He had to be joking. *Her?* Bewitch a man like *him*? A choked laugh escaped. 'Hardly!'

One arm curled around the bare flesh at her waist, sending a jolt of electricity coursing through her. He drew her against him, his free hand splayed between her shoulder blades, his fingers finding the skin left bare by her swim top. Their caress distracted her. Her own hands succumbed to temptation and slid up his muscled arms to rest on his shoulders—to keep some distance between them, she told herself. Nothing to do with how it felt to touch and savour the wet, warm, masculine flesh.

'Soon, *sirena mia*, you will tell me why you doubt yourself as a beautiful, sensual woman.'

'Rico—'

He leaned in, cutting off her protests with a kiss, stealing her breath and her reason. It began as gently and seductively as their first one, with Rico taking his time, teasing and tantalising until she was so restless and needy she wanted to beg him for more. But he knew…and he gave her what she craved, deepening the kiss, overwhelming her with his taste, and with the heat and force of the passion that raged so swiftly, leaving her boneless, beyond reason, drunk on him.

They swayed together with the buoyancy of the water, and Rico's knees slid between hers, a hand at the base of her spine urging her closer. Her breasts rubbed against his chest, the hardened peaks of her nipples so sensitive that the pleasure was almost too much to bear. Instinctively her legs wrapped around his hips, binding them more intimately. As her body pressed against his, making her intensely aware of his arousal, her fingers tightened their hold on supple flesh and firm muscle. Rico groaned. One arm was still locked around her, and his free hand glided down the side of her body, caressing the curve of one breast before journeying on so he could trail his fingers along the silken length of her thigh. His touch was like magic, and Ruth's breathlessness and trembling increased.

Hearing footsteps and voices drawing ever nearer, they broke the kiss a few moments before the spa lights flickered on, bring the intrusion of the outside world crashing into their solitude. Rico cradled her against him, refusing to let her go completely, and they drifted in the water, hearts racing in unison, breathing ragged. Ruth rested her head on his shoulder, aware of the clean male scent of him.

'They will start serving breakfast in half an hour,' one of the staff informed them.

Ruth felt Rico nod, aware he was sheltering her from view. 'Thank you.'

When they were alone again, he slowly relaxed his hold. The fire in his eyes conveyed his reluctance to bring their quiet interlude to an end, but he finally released her and vaulted out of the pool. Struggling to regain a measure of composure, Ruth watched the water sluicing off the perfect lines of his body. After tying a towel around his waist and draping another around his neck, he picked up her robe and held out his hand to her.

Shy and self-conscious, Ruth climbed out of the pool, feeling exposed and vulnerable. Every part of her quivered at the hunger with which he looked at her, his appreciation of her body, and in reaction to his touch as he slid on her robe. After tying the belt in a knot around her waist, he turned her round and drew her into his arms.

'I wish we could escape the rest of the conference, but we can't.' He drew back, his hands cupping her face, his expression intent. 'Please, stay, Ruth, after the final session is over. Give us time together to work everything out.'

This close to him she couldn't think clearly. What did he mean by 'everything'? She knew she should resist, should be sensible, but the temptation was immense and common sense seemed to have deserted her. So much so that she found herself nodding in agreement once more. Quite what she was agreeing to, she was too scared to ask.

Rico's smile, combined with the relief and promise in his eyes, turned her heart over in her chest. He dropped a lingering kiss on her mouth, then stepped back. 'Thank you, *sirena mia*. You won't regret it.'

Ruth hoped not. At the moment she wasn't sure what lay ahead and if she had just made a monumental mistake.

CHAPTER SIX

THE conference was over and nearly all the delegates had left. Yet Ruth remained, succumbing to Rico's appeal for more time and ignoring the whispering voice of reason in her head—a voice that was swiftly drowned out and overruled by the previously unknown part of her that wanted to be rebellious and adventurous.

Rico's suggestion of an after-dinner walk in the hotel's extensive private grounds, offering the chance for some fresh air and exercise to stretch her legs after hours in conference talks and activities, was welcome. She had thought it would buy her some time before anything too dangerous occurred and she was faced with the final decision on whether to stay or to go. She'd been right about the fresh air and exercise, but nothing lessened the electric tension or the intimacy whenever she was with him.

Hand in hand, they followed the circuitous path through the wood, the last rays of sunshine at the end of another glorious May day filtering low through the trees. Clouds of bluebells carpeted the ground with their lilac-blue trumpeted flowers and the still-warm air was perfumed with their delicious scent.

'Did you always want to be a doctor?' Rico asked, his fingers linked with hers and his hip brushing against her with every step making her constantly aware of him.

'Yes.' Ruth paused a moment and bit her lip, but the unfamiliar compulsion to tell him everything spurred her to continue. 'With both my parents involved in medicine, it was pretty much expected that I would be, too. Not that I would be a *GP*, however—that caused a lot of problems.'

He frowned, and she could hear the curiosity and puzzlement in his voice. 'What kind of problems?'

'My parents are well known in their respective fields and are also considered intellectually and academically brilliant. My father, Avery, is a professor of cardiology and my mother, Laura, is a research scientist, so I grew up in the kind of environment that expected the same success and achievement.'

What she told him was true, but she left out the

way she had felt pressured from a very young age to measure up—and never managing to. She also kept quiet about the fact that her parents were cold, undemonstrative people, unsuited for parenthood, and unable or unwilling to show her any love or affection. Not only had they withheld any affection from her, but she had never seen any sign of caring between them as a couple, either.

'They must be very proud of you.'

Ruth shrugged in response to Rico's statement. Unsettled, as she always was when thinking about her parents, she looked away, trying to ignore the memories that flooded back, the constant efforts to please them that had always ended in failure.

'Ruth?' Rico stopped walking and turned her to face him, his free hand cupping her chin so that his gaze could search hers. The gentle caress of his fingers was in contrast to the banked anger in his tone. 'Your parents did not support you?'

'They didn't agree with my choice and thought I should have worked harder, been better, achieved more. *We didn't raise you to accept the mediocre.*' It was a long-running argument,' she admitted, startled that she had confided so much in Rico.

'Being a GP and giving excellent health care

to people who need you is *not* mediocre.' Rico sounded both insistent and indignant. He raised their joined hands and pressed a kiss to the inside of her wrist, making her shiver at the sensation. 'You could *never* be mediocre, *sirena mia*, not in any way or anything you do.'

The sincerity of his words and the reality of his continued belief in her brought an uncharacteristic sting of tears to her eyes. She blinked them away. Why did she find Rico so easy to talk to? She was usually so reticent about her background, and had not even shared it all with Gina and Holly, the two best friends she'd ever had. But she had told Rico things she had never told anyone else. He understood her, and freely offered the approval and encouragement she had secretly always longed for.

He led her to a rustic wooden bench in a nearby clearing that offered a view of Morecambe Bay, retaining hold of her hand when they sat down. 'Ruth, if you want to remain a GP, if that is what makes you happy, then you must do so,' he began, his expression reflecting a range of emotions. 'But I asked you to come here on the strength of our email exchanges because I was so impressed with you… If things went well, my plan was to offer you a job.'

Ruth nodded when Rico paused. There was no point in pretending that the possibility had not occurred to her. She had anticipated it, part of her had wanted it, but she had never imagined to feel as she did about Rico when she met him. Now she remained silent and let him continue his explanation.

'You are an incredible doctor. And, selfishly, I want you to come and work with me. A switch to immunology would involve some initial retraining, but I am sure that would not cause you any problems. You have already picked up so much and stunned me with your ability to learn,' he told her with a knee-weakening smile. 'For the time being, it would also mean living and working in Florence. But just so you know where things are heading, I am in preliminary talks with a couple of NHS trusts about my plan to open a specialist clinic in the UK. My initial idea was to have you head up that new clinic.'

Ruth couldn't hide her surprise. 'Oh, my goodness! Really?' It was beyond her wildest dreams, and so flattering that Rico thought her capable.

'Really!' He chuckled at her reaction and then sobered again. 'I did some of my training in

London and hold the NHS in high regard. Colleagues in the UK have told me that specialist centres for allergy and immunology are thin on the ground, and patients with problems can wait ages for a proper diagnosis. Years in many cases.'

'Like Pippa Warren,' Ruth interjected.

'Exactly. A large proportion of doctors never see these immunological conditions, either during their training or once qualified, and so patients slip through the net. The lucky ones are caught before permanent damage is been done...but many are not.'

Ruth nodded, fascinated and excited by Rico's plans but also a little overwhelmed. 'We are seeing increasing numbers of people with allergies, too, and as a GP it is frustrating that there are not enough options open for me in terms of referring patients.'

'Is a change of specialty something you would be interested in?' Rico asked now. 'Would you consider it?'

She was more than tempted, but unsure how much of that was because of Rico himself. On the other hand, she had come here with this in mind before she had even met him in person, and surely she was professional enough to keep work in focus and ignore some misguided crush on the man who would be her boss.

But what of her youthful dream to be a GP? She had battled long and hard against her parents to achieve her goal. Yes, she had enjoyed her career and the interaction with her patients, but she had realised this last month that she was not being fully extended, and that was making her restless. As much as she loved Strathlochan, and her friends, she felt increasingly discontent at work. Were a junior partnership to be offered to her at the practice, she was not at all sure she would want to stay there, especially if it involved working with Graeme Campbell long term.

'Yes,' she found herself answering out loud, long before she had resolved any of the issues that worried her.

Rico's smile and the relief in his eyes took her breath away. 'Thank you. I know that contact with patients is important to you and you will still have that in allergy and immunology. As you have found with Pippa Warren, we work closely with our patients, often over long periods of time, and a great deal of detective work can be involved in making a diagnosis.'

'Everything I've learned has been fascinating.'

Ruth listened avidly as Rico gave her a brief

outline of just a few of the huge variety of cases he had seen this year alone in both adults and children. From rare conditions to the everyday food and substance intolerances, and numerous allergies, both familiar and unusual Ruth was fascinated.

'Just today my assistant emailed background details on a new patient referred to us—a woman aged forty who has developed an allergy to sunlight,' Rico explained, absently playing with her fingers. 'She has no previous history of allergic reactions or immune problems, but now has extreme photosensitivity which is keeping her housebound. She has swelling and rashes. And her skin blisters after the shortest time exposed to the sun. Even indoors. So the windows of her house have been covered. As soon as I return to Italy I will begin investigating the cause.'

Intrigued, Ruth felt a welling of eager excitement. She wanted to join the team in finding an answer to the puzzle—and the many others that she would be presented with if she changed specialty. It would be foolish to cling to her career as a GP just to prove a point to her parents. She was still young, and she had the rest of her life ahead of her to make her own decisions and do what she wanted. An inner knowledge and certainty grew that this change would bring her the most professional satisfaction and fulfilment. Of course, there was Rico... She had met him in person just the day before, and yet she felt an instinctive connection with him, as if they had known each other for ever—as if she had been waiting for him for ever.

'There is something else we must talk about,' he said, as if reading her mind. Ruth tensed. His eyes were full of warmth and sincerity, and his voice dropped to a sexy timbre that tightened the ache deep inside her. 'We cannot ignore the attraction between us, *sirena mia*. And I don't want to. But I must make it completely clear from the first that whatever is between us personally is separate from work. One is not dependent on the other. The job offer comes to you without any strings or expectations.'

'Rico—'

A finger pressed to her lips silenced her. 'Please, I need to say this. It is not something I expected when I asked you to come here. And I am breaking *all* my rules,' he added with a rueful and endearing smile. 'I have never had any kind of relationship with a colleague beyond the professional. The clinic and my work have taken over my life, so much so that I have not even been on a simple date for nearly two years,' he told her with surprising candour, leaving her speechless. His free hand settled over his heart, as if he was making a vow or a pledge. 'But, this, with you…I've *never* felt anything like it, Ruth. Not ever. The moment I looked at you I experienced the incredible connection between us, and that was before I knew who you were. Which was why I was shocked when I learned your identity—I knew there would be complications because of work. But not insurmountable ones.' Gentle fingers tucked a stray wisp of hair behind her ear, the brush of them against her skin making her tingle. 'I know it is scary, *sirena mia*—it is for me, too—but this feels too unique and important to ignore and leave unexplored.'

She might be the biggest fool on earth, but she looked into those captivating, gold-speckled hazel eyes and believed every word he said. Although unsure exactly what he was suggesting, one thing she did know…Rico was right, it *was* scary. More frightening than he could possibly know. But the searing attraction was too real, too strong and too exciting to be denied.

The pad of his thumb brushed the bare ring finger on her left hand. 'You are not already seeing anyone, Ruth?'

'No.'

Reality intruded into the fantasy and brought her crashing back to earth. All her insecurities and fears, and her belief that Adam had been right about her, flooded back to torment her. How could she have imagined, even for a second, that she could possibly please a man like Rico? All reason must have deserted her for her to ever get so carried away by foolish dreams.

Ruth pulled away and stood up, moving to stand with her back to him, staring out towards the expanse of sea as the sun began its descent towards the far horizon, layering the darkening skies with mauves and pinks and golds.

Rico frowned and tried to work out what had caused the sudden change in Ruth. He knew so much more about her now, as much from the things she had *not* said as those that she had. Coming from a home filled with love himself, the lack of care her parents had shown her made him furious. And his heart ached for her. He had glimpsed all too clearly the little girl trying so hard to be loved, to be good enough, to please, only to have it all thrown back in her face… rejected and unappreciated.

Yesterday evening she had spoken of how ostracised she had felt as a woman with brains, resented and misunderstood, including by some of her colleagues. No wonder she felt so alone. Few people had loved, supported and encouraged her in the past. But he wanted to do all those things and more, now and in the future— if only she would let him. He would show her how special she was. But first he had to find out what had upset her.

Rico rose to his feet, walked up behind her, and wrapped her in his arms, feeling the tension in her rigid frame. 'What is wrong, *sirena mia*?'

She shook her head, remaining unyielding in his hold. He nuzzled against her, breathing in her scent, lingering to brush a kiss to her neck and marvelling anew at the softness of her skin.

'Tell me, Ruth.' He felt a tremor ripple through her, and although he had yet to discover the cause of her anxiety, he sought to reassure her. 'There is nothing you could say that would change what I think of you or the respect I have for you.'

Or what I feel for you, he wanted to add, but knew it was too much too soon for her to hear that. She was way too skittish. How could he explain the depths of his feelings to her when he didn't understand them himself? If he told her about his father and Seb, about how they had met their soul mates and had known instantly it was right, would she believe he was sincere and that *she* was *his*? He believed, yet it sounded crazy even to him, so how could he expect Ruth to understand so soon?

Rico waited as dusk continued to roll in, wanting so much for Ruth to trust him. Silence stretched and he forced himself to be patient. Then he felt something wet drip onto his wrist. *Dio!* He turned her round and cupped her face, the fading light failing to hide the tears that shimmered in her incredible green eyes.

'Ruth… Do not cry, *sirena mia*, I cannot bear it. Please, tell me what is wrong. Let me help.'

'You can't.' The words whispered from her before she took a ragged breath. Then her voice strengthened. 'I don't understand what's happening. I don't *do* this.' She sounded endearingly confused and flustered by something so strong and yet beyond her control. 'I'm no good. Not a siren at all. You've made a mistake. I'll just be a letdown to you.'

Her statement stunned him and was so absurd he wanted to laugh. But he didn't because Ruth clearly believed what she had said. Despite being mature and supremely intelligent, a caring doctor who exuded professional competence, something was affecting her inner confidence as a woman. Something serious that he needed to understand and address.

'I promise that you will *never* be a letdown, and most certainly not to me.' He cuddled her close. 'But why do you think this, Ruth? What—or who,' he amended, recalling the fragmented clues he'd gleaned in the last two days, 'makes you say it?'

For several moments he thought she was not going to speak, then she unconsciously pressed against him, her arms curling around his waist as she released a shaky sigh. He tightened his hold, offering comfort and support.

'I was at an all-girls' boarding school until I was eighteen. It was OK but I was different and I didn't have any real friends. Aside from swimming, my whole life revolved around study,' she explained hesitantly. Rico slid one hand beneath her hair and caressed her neck, needing the contact as he waited for her to continue. 'I went straight to medical school and again threw myself into learning—it's what I enjoy, what I know. The socialising was new to me. I felt awkward, always on the outside. Everybody was pairing up. Adam was the only person to ask me out. I'm ashamed to say that I fell into a relationship with him partly because it was expected and partly because I so desperately wanted to fit in, to be accepted, to be like everyone else.'

A lump lodged in Rico's throat. How alone Ruth must have felt, especially as she had not known any love at home or formed any close friendships at school. 'There is nothing to be ashamed of, *carissima*,' he corrected, hearing the emotion that roughened his voice as he tried to convince her that he understood.

'At first Adam seemed pleased that I wasn't "high maintenance", as he called it, and needing attention. He liked playing football and drinking with his friends, while I appreciated having the space and the quiet so that I could study. Besides, I—'

Ruth abruptly stopped speaking and ducked her head, as if embarrassed. He slid his hand round from her nape to capture her chin and tilt her face back up. Her lashes lifted to reveal anxious green eyes. The last of the light was fading, but he made no attempt to move or return to the hotel, anxious not to break the mood now that Ruth was sharing something he knew was vitally important from her past.

'You, what?' he encouraged softly.

She bit her lip in indecision. 'I never enjoyed the physical side of things,' she whispered, her lashes lowering again to mask her expression.

Rico took a moment to compose himself. 'Did he hurt you?'

'No.'

The reply was too quick, and he held his breath, concerned at what she might yet reveal. 'Ruth?'

'He didn't hurt me...not physically,' she finally admitted, and he released the breath he'd been holding, although relief was tempered by the realisation that the man had harmed her in some other way.

'What happened, *sirena mia*? What did he do?'

'He resented that the study came easily to me, that I worked hard and passed exams with little apparent struggle. Adam barely scraped through them.' She paused, resting her forehead on his shoulder. 'When we went our separate ways, I vowed never to repeat the experience. Especially given what Adam said.'

A cold knot formed in Rico's stomach. 'What *did* he say?' he prompted, one arm still locked around her, his free hand stroking the silken fall of her hair. A shudder ran through her. 'Ruth...?'

Before he could prepare himself, she began

speaking again. 'Adam's parting words were: *"There is nothing remotely sexual, appealing or attractive about you, Ruth. You're unresponsive, cold and frigid, and you don't give me any pleasure. You might pass your exams with distinction, but you're a total failure as a woman."* Then he left,' she finished, with a strangled sound halfway between a laugh and a sob.

'*Bastardo.*'

A furious rage rose inside him, completely out of character and at odds with his easygoing nature. Rico wanted to confront the man who had done this to Ruth. He hurt for her, imagining what a fatal blow it must have been to her already shaky self-esteem, especially when she had no other experiences to counterbalance the lies, and no one to whom she was close who could boost her confidence.

And in all the time since those words had been fired at her she had never allowed herself to get close to anyone and had believed the cruel and untrue things that man had said? Rico closed his eyes and cradled her against him, needing to keep her safe and protected. Ruth had shut herself off from love, believing she wasn't good enough, thinking she was a failure as a woman. No wonder she had been thrown off balance by the electric connection and blaze of passion they had shared from the moment they had met.

It was a testament to how amazing Ruth was that she had come through her childhood with unloving parents, her years in a friendless boarding school, and then her experience with Adam, to emerge so grounded, so strong, still so caring and compassionate, and still with a sense of fun and an ability to set other people at ease, even in situations that made her uncomfortable. Admiration and love churned inside him. Rico planned to show her just how special and beautiful, attractive and arousing she was…and he wanted to reinforce that message every day for the rest of their lives.

He drew in an unsteady breath. Once again he was getting ahead of himself. The first step was to convince Ruth that everything Adam had said was nonsense. And the best way to do that was to take her to bed and prove just how sensual, sexy, feminine and wonderful she was, and just how much pleasure she could receive and give. He had one night to show her how magical things could be between them—one night to win her round to accept him in every way, professionally and personally.

* * *

Rico was silent for so long that Ruth began to worry that confiding in him had been a mistake. Not that she had told him *everything*. She remembered Adam's verbal assault word for word, but she had not been able to voice aloud his sneering taunt about her inability to achieve an orgasm. For a moment she closed her eyes, reliving the humiliation of their final moments together.

Pushing the memories aside, she leaned against Rico and wondered what he was thinking. Would he reject her now that he knew she was a failure? What was it about this man that stripped away her defences and had her telling him things she had never told another living soul? It had been happening from the first moment they had met. In two days he knew more about her life, her past, her dreams and her insecurities than anyone else. And no matter what she had told him, he had never wavered, had never laughed at her, and had not given the slightest sign that he thought any less of her. Quite the opposite, in fact. He gave her his undivided attention, he listened as if what she said mattered and was important to him, and he made her feel valued and respected.

He also made her feel safe and yet in terrible

danger. Like now—cocooned in his embrace. She welcomed his comfort and strength, was soothed by his steady heartbeat and his cedar-wood scent. Yet all the time she was aware of the charged awareness and the ache of want that never went away. Ruth sighed, relaxing into him. It was far too comfortable being right there in his arms with him holding her as if he would never let her go.

After an endless time he drew back, and she felt the loss as his arms released her. But then his hands cupped her face, his expression impossible to read in the gathering darkness. He moved closer until his lips brushed hers, teasing and tantalising for a breathtaking moment until her own parted and he deepened the kiss. Reality was swept away as the passion ignited, and Ruth clung to him, lost in the firestorm, matching his demands, making her own, savouring his taste as his tongue invaded and invited hers to duel and dance. He nibbled and sucked on each lip in turn, then drew her tongue into the moist heat of his mouth.

She moaned in protest as the unexpected but fiercely erotic kiss ended far too soon, thankful for the arm around her waist as her legs were far too weak and wobbly to support her on their own. Her heart thundered in her chest and it was an effort to pull each breath into her lungs.

'You believe you are unresponsive when we kiss?' Rico demanded, his sexy, accented voice husky and rough. One hand fisted in her hair, keeping her gaze locked with his. 'You believe you do not feel pleasure yourself or give pleasure to me?' Ruth gasped as his other hand shaped the swell of her rear and pulled her closer, his hips rocking against hers so that she felt his undeniable arousal. 'You believe I don't want and desire you, that I don't find you sexy and attractive, *sirena mia*? What of the way we both explode with the intensity of the passion we share?'

'Rico…' She was so stunned and breathless that she could barely force out his name, let alone form a coherent sentence.

Her whole body was trembling as he took her hand in his and led her back along the woodland path, the lights of the hotel a beacon in the darkness. She was too bemused and nervous to ask where they were going. Neither of them spoke as they crossed the deserted foyer, and neither paid any attention to the hum of chatter and laughter coming from the restaurant and bar. Bypassing the lift, their footsteps whispered up the richly carpeted main stairway. Ruth's fingers tightened on Rico's as they ignored the floor that housed her room and climbed two more flights before he opened a door and they moved onto a quiet landing. Near the end of the corridor a turn led to a solitary suite. Rico released her hand, unlocked the door and stepped inside before turning back to face her, his gaze intent, his voice serious.

'Tomorrow the world will intrude again. You will have to return to your surgery, and I have some family commitments I cannot ignore before I can return to Italy. Tomorrow we can exchange addresses and arrange a time—hopefully very soon—for you to come to Florence, to look around the clinic and talk about the job.' He paused, looking uncharacteristically nervous, and Ruth held her breath. When he continued, his voice was smoky and rough and sent tingles down her spine. 'Tonight is ours alone. Give me this time to show you how magical it will be for us, to prove to you that everything that cowardly and jealous man said to you was a lie, and to convince you that you are an exciting, desirable and sensual woman... beautiful and sexy and *never* a letdown. What do you say, *sirena mia*?'

In the silence that followed, Ruth could hear every thud of her heart, and she struggled to remember how to breathe. She met the intensity of Rico's gaze as he waited for her to make a decision. Should she play safe and go? Or stay— and face a night beyond her wildest imaginings?

Rico made her feel special and wanted as never before. There was a hollow place inside her that craved fulfilment and understanding, a part of her that yearned for approval and desperately wanted to belong. It had been there all her life and she had tried unsuccessfully to fill it by throwing all her energies into work. But Rico made her feel less hollow, less alone. Just once in her life she wanted to experience what it was like to be desired.

What if she turned him down now and never had the chance for the rest of her life to experience anything like it again? The temptation was too great to resist. She had never felt like this with anyone else. Yes, he overwhelmed her senses. Yes, he had seduced her with his charm and his magnetism, his sexy voice and the hunger in his eyes. But if this was to go further, it was to be her decision, her choice. He was giving her free will, but also responsibility.

She knew a price would have to be paid afterwards, but maybe it would be worth it. And maybe she had subconsciously made her decision when she had agreed to stay the extra night. Scared and excited, Ruth stepped into the room and sealed her fate.

'Thank you.' He sounded relieved and sincere, and the warm promise in his voice fired her blood. 'I will do all I can to ensure you have no regrets.'

After locking the door, he guided her through the suite to the bedroom. Ruth's heart nearly stopped when she saw the huge four-poster bed that dominated the plush room. 'Oh, my.' She only realised she had murmured the words aloud when she heard Rico's wry chuckle.

'I am not normally one for ostentatious luxuries and I was surprised when I arrived here to discover I had been assigned an executive bedroom,' he told her, crossing the room to close the curtains.

Uncertain what to do, a whole squadron of butterflies fluttering in her stomach, Ruth hovered anxiously in the bedroom as Rico disappeared into the adjoining bathroom, returning moments later with a satin-lined wicker basket.

'This I barely glanced at, never expecting to use it,' he said, setting his treasure on the bedside chest. 'Now I am grateful for the hotel's welcome gifts.'

As Rico switched on the two bedside lamps, Ruth had a quick peep into the basket, spotting, amongst other things, massage oil and an unopened box of condoms. She turned round as the main light was extinguished, leaving the room cast in the warm muted glow of the lamps. Her breath lodged in her throat as Rico closed the gap between them, halting in front of her.

'Take off my clothes.'

The instruction was issued in a husky whisper, the words beguiling, shocking and seducing her. Rico made no move to touch her, or to force her compliance. If she wanted this, wanted *him*, he was not going to allow her to be a passive by-stander. For a moment all her fears and inadequacies rose up, daunting her. She had made a terrible mistake. She couldn't do this. Knowing every emotion must be reflected in her eyes, she met Rico's gaze. Seeing the trust and desire there boosted her flagging confidence.

Fingers shaking so badly she struggled to control them, she slowly undid the buttons down the front of his crisp white shirt, exposing tantalising glimpses of olive-toned skin as she went. She bit her lip as she pulled the tails of the shirt free of the waistband of his trousers, her mouth watering as she eased the material off his shoulders and down his arms, her gaze greedily savouring the lean, sculpted musculature of his torso.

A subtle hint of warm cedar mingled with the musky maleness of him and left her heady. She yearned to touch him, but she still felt cautious and unsure of herself, so she sucked in a shaky breath and turned her attention back to her task. Her hands were even more clumsy as they unsnapped his belt, then moved to the fastening of his trousers, but Rico did no more than toe off his shoes and wait for her to continue at her own pace.

As she undid the button and eased down the zipper, her fingers brushed against his arousal. He drew in a sharp breath, reacting instantly to her touch, his stomach muscles clenching. Focused on him and the perfection of his body, some of her awkwardness dissipated, and she slowly drew down the fabric of his trousers, taking his briefs with them, leaving him standing before her, naked and proud. Her heart hammered in her chest and she was unable to drag her gaze from the sight of him, acknowledging his magnificence while at the same time experiencing a flicker of fear at his raw sexuality and blatant maleness.

This wasn't her, Ruth worried. She didn't do this. She'd never enjoyed sex before, and even though everything was so different with Rico, and she had responded to him so readily, what if she *was* a failure and couldn't please him? Despite being the one fully clothed, she felt incredibly defenceless and insecure. Her gaze inched back up until it met his again and she saw the understanding there, mixed with the heated desire.

'Now undress for me, Ruth.'

She couldn't! The almost imperceptible shake of her head and her startled gasp betrayed her anxiety. She wanted to move away but her feet refused to obey her. Rico's compelling eyes gleamed with knowledge, promise and a burning hunger that had her blood racing crazily through her veins. There was nothing to bind her. Nothing but that sinful gaze and sexy voice. Yet freedom was an illusion…she was captive to the desire, to the clawing need that intensified inside her.

Trembling, she began to take off her clothes, self-conscious, yet warmed by the appreciation in Rico's eyes as he followed her every movement, all but devouring each part of her she uncovered. By the time she had removed her ankle boots, socks, jacket and trousers, she still felt acutely nervous, but a strange sensation of power was creeping in as she observed the effect her inexpert striptease was having on Rico. Taking her time, more from nervousness than from a conscious effort to tantalise, she drew her jersey over her head, and then summoned the courage to remove the final garments…a pale green lacy bra and matching panties. As they fluttered from her fingers to the floor, Rico's breath hitched, his eyes darkened further, and she could see the rapid pulse beat in his neck.

He still hadn't touched her, yet his hot, hungry gaze felt like a caress. A quiver ran through her. She had never had any particular hang-ups about her body, believing it to be fairly average and ordinary, but the unmistakable appreciation and hunger Rico displayed as he looked at her made her feel special and beautiful for the first time in her life…and not average and ordinary at all.

Rico held out his hand, and Ruth took an unsteady step forward, feeling completely vulnerable and exposed as she slipped her hand into his. She trusted him, but that didn't stop the tension and anxiety returning as she questioned her ability to satisfy him and to enjoy what was to come. To her surprise, after a light, teasing and far-too-short kiss, Rico had her lie face down on the bed, and she turned her head to see what he was doing, nervous and excited.

He took the massage oil from the basket and warmed some in his hands. A sound somewhere between a gasp, a moan and a sigh escaped unchecked as he touched her. Rico was in no hurry, and his gliding, caressing hands were magical, almost reverent, making her feel cherished as they soothed and stimulated, teasing the tightness out of the muscles in her back and shoulders while at the same time learning and exploring her body. Her arms, legs and the cheeks of her rear enjoyed the same slow, erotic attention, and by the time he was finished, Ruth felt boneless, incredibly relaxed and yet aroused beyond bearing.

But Rico was not yet done. After turning her on her back, he began a lingering, torturous journey from her feet, up the length of her legs, bypassing the female heart of her that desperately craved his touch. He used just the right amount of pressure low on her belly, over the point where the aching knot of want grew tighter and heavier. Journeying on, a combination of light and firm strokes in a circular caress around her navel, had her begging for a more intimate touch.

Ruth didn't recognise herself. She was stunned at her reactions, at the sounds she made in response to his touch. Then, when she thought she couldn't bear it any more, he took her to a higher level of pleasure and arousal as his wicked, skilful hands lavished attention of her breasts...still slow, still judging just how and where to touch, until she thought she was going to explode. Nothing could be better than this. But then he proved her wrong again, inching back down to settle between her trembling thighs and doing impossible, unimagined things with his mouth and his fingers that blasted her straight into the stratosphere.

Crying out, she clung to Rico as her first proper orgasm with a man had her soaring to the heavens. Extending and prolonging her release, he held her as she flew into space, keeping her safe, and wiping her tears of joy as she came slowly back to earth, a series of aftershocks rippling through her.

'I couldn't... I've never...' Her breathless, awkward words trailed off, unable to voice just what this had meant to her. She forced herself to open her eyes, seeing understanding and recognition in his own. 'Thank you.'

'Thank you for sharing something so special

and wonderful with me.' He kissed her, his lips trailing around her neck. 'You are amazing, *sirena mia,*' he murmured against her ear, nipping and sucking on her lobe. 'So beautiful, so sensual.'

'I should give you a massage now,' Ruth told him, wanting to experience everything.

He shook his head and kissed her. 'Not this time. I'm too close to the edge. And this night is all about you and your pleasure.'

Ruth had no time to be disappointed at not being able to explore Rico's body as he had hers because she was soon lost in sensation as his hands and his mouth took her back to paradise. He kissed her all over, his unshaven jaw a delicious caress over her super-sensitive skin as he lavished attention from the top of her head to the tips of her toes and back again, lingering at her breasts, tormenting each proud, aroused crest until she thought she would expire from the overload of pleasure.

When the time came, Rico encouraged her to help him with the condom, guiding her fingers as she learned the feel and shape and texture of him. Her confidence increased and she lost her inhibitions, her hands roving over his body, hungry and greedy, as his own caresses brought her up to yet another peak.

Ruth was unable to hold back tears at the beauty of the moment when he finally joined his body with hers, overwhelmed by the incredible intimacy, the shocking, earth-shattering ecstasy. Throughout it all, Rico's husky whispered words told her how special she was, how incredible she felt, how wonderful she made him feel. And then neither of them had the breath to talk. Together they plunged over the edge of the precipice and spiralled into the abyss, her cries mingling with his as wave after wave of pleasure, even greater than before, crashed through her.

'I'll never forget tonight,' she murmured eventually, sated and overwhelmed.

A husky rumble sounded in her ear. 'We have only just begun, *sirena mia.*'

With a sexy, wicked, bad-boy smile, Rico turned her in his arms and proceeded to show her just what he had in mind…again and again and again.

CHAPTER SEVEN

'THANK you so much, Dr Baxter. I was really scared, but seeing a female doctor made me a lot more comfortable.' Rhona Nairn, a slim twenty-one-year-old, readjusted her clothing. 'You've been so kind and reassuring. You, too, Nurse Neason.'

Washing her hands, Ruth smiled at the young woman who was the penultimate patient on her Friday afternoon list. 'We're glad to help,' Ruth replied, thankful that the procedure she had just performed had been quick and trouble-free.

'That's what we're here for, lovey,' Esther Neason agreed, patting Rhona on the shoulder before she returned her attention to tidying the treatment room. 'Anything else I can do, Doctor?'

'I'd be grateful if you could make sure that the sample is sent off to the pathology lab without delay,' Ruth requested, checking a final time that the correct details were on the label of the container which held the excised tissue in a solution of formalin to preserve it.

'No problem.' The practice nurse smiled as she bustled about the room. 'I'll see to it myself and make sure it goes straight away.'

'Thanks, Esther.'

Ruth always enjoyed working with the older woman because Esther was efficient and calm, and she had a gentle way with patients. She was also the person who had made her most welcome when she had joined the practice, Ruth reflected, recalling the many times she had been grateful for the matronly nurse's kind words and quiet understanding. With Rhona ready, Ruth thanked Esther again, then led her patient back to her consulting room.

'What causes cervical polyps, Dr Baxter?' Rhona asked as she sat down a few moments later.

'The cause isn't completely understood. They might be due to an injury, congestion in the cervical blood vessels, or because of increased levels of oestrogen. Another theory is that they may arise after an infection and accompanying inflammation. They grow from a mucous membrane, and can be found in many other parts of the body, such as the nose, ear or stomach.

Some women have no symptoms at all with a cervical polyp, while others have bleeding between periods and after intercourse…as you did,' Ruth explained after she had finished typing up instructions for a prescription for Rhona. 'Usually they are quickly removed. Yours was a single polyp that was easy to access, which is why I was able to remove it and cauterise the root straight away.'

Rhona nodded, her brow knotted in concentration. 'Will it come back?'

'It's uncommon for them to recur. And it's almost certainly benign. The vast majority of cervical polyps are. But we send them for testing just to be one hundred per cent sure.' Ruth stressed the point, wanting to make certain that the young woman understood and was not unduly anxious. 'The result from your test should be back in seven to ten days, but I don't want you to worry, Rhona…conducting the test is standard procedure and *not* a sign of anything more serious.'

'That's OK, Dr Baxter. I feel much calmer now.' Rhona smiled, running the fingers of one hand through her short ginger hair.

Ruth was pleased to have been able to identify and relieve Rhona's problem so swiftly. 'I'm glad. Now, I'm going to give you a course of antibiotics to counteract any possible infection.' The prescription emerged from the printer and Ruth signed it before handing it over.

'Thanks so much.'

'My pleasure,' Ruth assured her. 'If you have any questions, don't hesitate to call. I'm away for the next two weeks, but Dr Catriona Robson, one of the senior partners, will be here and you can ask to speak to her if you find that easier.'

After Rhona had gone, Ruth wrote up her notes, feeling increasingly edgy as the time for her final appointment approached. It was a consultation that had been arranged over a week ago and Ruth had scheduled it for the last slot so that she would not be rushed and could take some extra time if it was needed. She set down her pen, unable to concentrate. Any moment now Judith Warren would arrive, eager to hear whatever additional information and advice Ruth had been able to glean at the conference about CVID and how it might affect young Pippa.

Thinking about the conference, the Warrens and CVID made her think about Rico.

As if she didn't think about him all the time.

Ruth covered her face with her hands as wave

after wave of turbulent emotions crashed through her. She was amazed she had survived the last three days. Somehow she had managed to appear outwardly calm, but everything inside her was in turmoil, and the only way she had made it through each minute, each hour and each day had been by throwing herself into her work. By keeping busy she hoped to stop herself thinking. By keeping busy she could try to forget the most incredible experience of her life…and her guilt at having run away.

Because there was no escaping the fact that running away was exactly what she had done. Panicked, overwhelmed, scared and unsure, she had taken the coward's way out because she had not known how to handle the situation. And now she felt ashamed, as well as guilty. Not to mention even more confused than she had been when she had woken up before dawn on Wednesday morning, her limbs entangled with Rico's, her head pillowed on his chest.

A ragged breath shuddered out of her lungs as she looked back at her magical night with him and what had happened since.

Her time with Rico had been beyond anything she could ever have imagined and he had far surpassed everything he had promised her. In one night he had swept away years of pain and torment caused by the words that had shattered her self-esteem and wounded her so deeply. Rico had proved in no uncertain terms that with him, at least, she was sexual and wanton and insatiable, and not only could she give him extreme pleasure but she could enjoy multiple orgasms herself.

At first, the intensity and explosive passion of their wildly erotic time together had shocked her, but Rico had refused to allow her to be shy. After he had relaxed her with the slow, sensual massage and then taken her to paradise for the first time, he had spent much of the rest of the night coaxing out an uninhibited side she had never known she had. He had encouraged her to give all of herself, and had given everything of himself in return. She couldn't believe the liberties she had allowed him to take, or what she had done with him and to him. He had made her feel vulnerable but incredibly alive as he had taken over her body and shaken her to her very foundations. He had also made her feel powerful as a woman able to pleasure a man. *Her* man.

And therein lay the root of the problem. Rico was not her man. He had offered her an unforgettable night out of time and she had taken it.

She had known there would be a price to pay for it, and had believed she could handle it. But she couldn't. Not now she knew what the cost would be. Because now she had had a taste of paradise, one night was not enough. She wanted more. All of Rico. For ever.

Was it possible to fall in love in two days? Never having experienced these feelings before, Ruth wasn't sure. But when she had woken in Rico's arms after very little sleep, she had looked at him and had known deep inside that this man had changed her and that her heart and her body and her soul were bound to his. Fearful at the way her life had been turned upside down and knowing she could never let Rico discover her feelings, she had slipped out of his bed, out of his room and, quite possibly, she had thought at that moment, out of his life.

Rico had promised her a special night, and those magical hours with him had changed her in some fundamental and irrevocable way. Her body no longer felt as if it belonged to her. She didn't know herself. Scared and confused, she had hurried back to her room and collected her things. Downstairs, she had met the night porter still on duty who had told her that her bill had already been paid on her behalf. Not wanting to argue, needing only to escape, she had rushed to her car, tossed her things inside and had started her drive home as the first rays of sunshine were breaking through.

She had not been able to stop thinking about Rico or wanting him since. And she had not properly considered how leaving that way might affect him until she had seen the email that had been awaiting her when she had first logged on after arriving home.

'You frightened me, Ruth. What happened to make you leave that way? Please, if nothing else for now, let me know that you are safe.'

That was when the guilt and shame had joined all the other emotions vying for dominance within her. 'I'm sorry. I had to get back for work. I need to think.'

Her reply had only made her feel worse. But then Rico had written again, and his words had stayed with her, leaving her uncertain and not knowing what to do.

'I will honour your need for some time, *sirena mia*. I cannot lie—I was upset to wake up and discover you had gone. And I do not plan to let things end here. But I have family commitments I must attend to now. So by all means think, *carissima*, but please, do not deny the last few days. You have my mobile number. You can phone, text or email me at any time. I will not push you now, but I will be in touch once the family business is completed, and arrange for you to come to Italy and see the clinic as agreed. And if you are missing your locket, do not worry, I found it in the bathroom. I will keep it safe until I can return it to you. Soon, *sirena mia*.'

Ruth's unsteady hand settled at her throat, which felt bare without the locket that meant so much to her. But remembering what had happened in that hotel bathroom and why Rico had taken the locket off had her cheeks flushing and her whole body flaring with heat and need. Yes, she felt the loss of the locket, but she also felt a huge sense of loss without Rico. They had shared an unforgettable night. Everything in her had wanted to beg for more but, fearing rejection, she had run, leaving her heart behind her.

Rico's email suggested that he thought they could go on as before, as if their incredibly sensual night had never happened. How could she consider taking the job with Rico now? To see him all the time, to work with him and never be able to touch him would be agonising. But she would be a fool to turn down such a wonderful career opportunity, one that filled her with enthusiasm and which would challenge and stimulate her as no other.

How could two days—and one phenomenal night—have changed her and her life so radically? She had gone into it with her eyes open, had accepted the terms, and she couldn't now change the rules. When they met again, as Rico determined they would, it would be as professionals, colleagues, with Rico as her potential boss.

The ring of her phone brought an abrupt end to Ruth's troubled thoughts. 'Judith Warren is here, Dr Baxter,' receptionist Janet Dalyrmple informed her crisply. Two years on and the woman remained very much the cheerleader of Graeme Campbell's supporters.

'Thank you, Janet, please send her through,' Ruth responded politely, refusing to react to her surliness.

A few moments later Judith appeared. Smiling, Ruth invited her to sit down, then she drew in a deep breath, struggling to mask her personal feelings as she told the concerned mother all the information she had gathered about CVID and passed on to her the advice Rico had given.

'I'm so grateful to you. You've put in so much

effort on our behalf,' Judith praised as Ruth showed her out half an hour later. 'We were in such a rut before we saw you. It doesn't help that my husband's job takes him away for weeks at a time. He isn't here to see all that Pippa goes through, and at times I think he wondered if I *was* imagining things, as the other doctors suggested. Now, for the first time in years, someone believes in us and we really feel there is light at the end of the tunnel for Pippa.'

Embarrassed, Ruth shook the woman's hand. 'It's my job, and I am just pleased I could help.'

'It's much more than that. No one else did anything for us. Thank you.'

Ruth felt uncharacteristically emotional as Judith left. She had been on a knife edge the whole time she was talking to the older woman, because all she had been able to hear in her head had been Rico's voice as she had repeated his words. He had given his undivided attention to Pippa's case. And the support he had shown, his belief in *her*, had been the turning point that had started the changes that had taken place inside her this last week. Ruth pressed a clenched fist to her sternum where the ever-present ache gripped tighter than ever.

After finishing her notes, putting everything in

order so there were no loose ends during her two weeks' holiday, Ruth headed to the staff-room, thankful to find it empty. She couldn't wait to get home. She had promised to look after Gina's dog, a bouncy black Labrador called Montgomery, for the duration of the honeymoon and now, with so much on her mind, she was glad she had gone the whole hog and had taken some of the time off that was owing to her.

'I see you've been stealing more of my patients, Ruth.'

The snide remark from behind her alerted Ruth to Graeme Campbell's unwelcome presence. Stifling a groan, she finished putting on her coat and turned round, watching as the unpleasant man swaggered into the room, reminding her of one of the main reasons a change in career was so appealing. Seeing the sneer on his face, Ruth lifted her chin and stared him down.

'I wasn't aware they belonged to you, Graeme,' she responded with an inner calmness that surprised her.

From the corner of her eye, she saw a couple of senior doctors and the practice manager enter the room, but they were behind Graeme and he had yet to notice their arrival or to realise that his outburst was being witnessed.

'Rhona Nairn sees *me*. Remember that. You are not queen bee around here.' Graeme accompanied the statement with an aggressive move forward, pointing a finger close to her.

'I understood that it was practice policy to encourage patients to see whomever they choose.' Ruth sidestepped Graeme and put some distance between them. 'Rhona asked for an appointment with a woman doctor and she was assigned to my list. If you have a problem with that, I suggest you discuss it with David. I've put up with your rudeness, your disrespect and your petty harassment for two years, Graeme,' she continued, her voice calm and controlled. 'Be warned that I am not prepared to tolerate them any more.'

She had never spoken up to Graeme before and that she had done so now appeared to surprise him and deflate some of his bluster.

'Is there a problem here, Ruth?' one of her senior colleagues asked.

Again she raised her chin and, ignoring the nervous fluttering in her stomach, she held Graeme's angry gaze. 'No problem. Unless Graeme wants to make one.'

Her antagonist grunted, looking as if he wanted to say more, but not daring to.

Ruth gave a brief, cool smile. 'Good. I think we understand each other.'

With a muffled curse, Graeme stamped out of the room like a thwarted schoolboy, the door to his consulting room slamming shut seconds later. Maintaining her composure, although her heart was thudding under her ribs, Ruth turned to face the colleagues who had witness the altercation. Before she could apologise, however, Bruce Tonner, the second in command at the surgery, surprised her by chuckling.

'We should send you off to conferences more often, if this is the effect it has on you, Ruth!' he told her.

Ruth frowned. 'How do you mean?'

'You've come back from Lancashire a changed woman. Very feisty!' He smiled, pale blue eyes twinkling. 'It's about time you stood up to Graeme. Good for you.'

Ruth was still puzzled as Bruce left the room.

'He's right, you know,' practice manager Jilly Sheldon commented, stirring a teaspoon of sugar into the mug of tea she had just poured herself. 'Graeme deserved it—he's had it coming a long time.'

'Hear, hear,' Peter Hemming, another senior GP, agreed.

Perching on the arm of a nearby chair, Jilly smiled at her. 'I don't know what happened to you in England, Ruth, but the change in you has been apparent ever since you came back two days ago. You even walk differently.'

'I do?'

'Yes.' Jilly sipped her tea, her gaze speculative. 'Your head is up and you exude a new confidence.'

Ruth was shocked at the observations. Lost in thought, she picked up her bag, said goodnight, and walked out of the surgery to her car. The cool, damp air met her overheated cheeks. Astounded with herself for facing up to Graeme, and equally surprised that her colleagues had noticed changes in her, she drove home. Since Wednesday, she had been so locked in her inner turmoil that she had been unaware of the differences Bruce, Peter and Jilly claimed to see. It was true, she never would have confronted Graeme like that before. But she knew where her new-found confidence had come from. Rico.

A fresh wave of pain lanced through her. What was she going to do? Ruth had no answers to that question as she pulled into the drive of her secluded cottage outside town.

Somehow she had to get through the next twenty-four hours. Tonight she would be with

Gina and Holly, and she didn't want her friends to know that anything was wrong. Tomorrow morning Gina was getting married and nothing could spoil her special day, Ruth vowed as she let herself into her house. She went through to the kitchen, filled the kettle and switched it on, craving a reviving cup of tea.

After the wedding she would have two weeks to herself. Two weeks in which to do some serious thinking and make up her mind what to do—about her career and about Rico.

A shiver rippled through her. Why did she have a sudden premonition that something was about to happen?

Hands thrust into his trouser pockets, Rico stared sightlessly out of the window and into the darkness of the night.

'You are miles away, *cugino*. What is so interesting out there?'

Sighing, Rico closed the curtains and turned round, looking at Seb who was sitting across the room on the settee, two of the household's cats vying for prime position on his lap. '*Scusami*. I am sorry.'

Rico sat back down in the armchair he had recently vacated and brushed his palms over his face. He couldn't deny his cousin's gentle accusation—he was preoccupied. The last sixty-two hours had passed in a blur of disappointment, anxiety and uncertainty. Now it was ten o'clock on Friday night, and his hosts, Nic and Hannah, had just gone up to bed after the four of them had shared a quiet but enjoyable dinner. Seb, who was getting married the next day, was also staying over, tradition decreeing that he should not see his bride again until she walked down the aisle.

Rico took his role as best man seriously, but right now his mind was elsewhere…back in a hotel room overlooking Morecambe Bay, where he had woken at seven o'clock on Wednesday morning, after the most incredible night of his life, to discover that Ruth had vanished.

He had been devastated. Angry. Hurt. Confused. Worried. There had been a vast range of emotions bubbling inside him since the reality had sunk in that Ruth had gone. No note. No message. And no details about where he could find her. All he had was her email address. Accepting the inevitable—that Ruth was *not* coming back—he had driven up, as arranged, to be with his cousin in Scotland, where final preparations for the wedding had been in full swing.

There had to be something in the Scottish air,

Rico mused. The last time he had been here had been for Nic and Hannah's wedding. And now, six years later, he was here for Seb's. The location was beautiful, the scenery magnificent, and the way of life relaxed. Rico had enjoyed his time here in the past, but now he could not wind down or stop his mind working overtime on ways to find and reclaim Ruth.

He'd only been with her for two days, but he missed her. He wanted her, ached for her, was unable to sleep without her. After their magical night together he had thought that the major hurdle had been crossed. But he'd been wrong. Foolishly complacent. His hand slid into his trouser pocket, his fingers curling around Ruth's platinum chain and the delicate locket suspended upon it. He'd found it in the bathroom on Wednesday morning. A ragged sigh escaped as he recalled the exact moment during their deliciously erotic night when he had taken it off and set it aside for safe-keeping before drawing her under the shower, soaping her beautiful body from head to toe, and then making love to her again.

'What is wrong, *cugino*?' Seb asked, and Rico looked up to see that his cousin was looking at him with concern. 'You have been troubled since you arrived on Wednesday. Is it work?'

'No. I—' He broke off, unsure what to say, where to start.

Seb's dark brown eyes widened in sudden perception. '*Accidenti*! I don't believe it. You've met someone!'

'What if I have?' he countered defensively, dragging his free hand through his hair.

'Then I would be thrilled. Surprised, since you have never shown any sign of being serious about a woman, nor have you even dated for ages, so dedicated have you been to the clinic, but thrilled.' Seb paused a moment, his expression growing reflective. 'But you do not look happy. Who is she, Rico? What has happened?'

Expelling a shaky breath, Rico leaned forward, resting his elbows on his knees. 'I'm going to sound just like you eight months ago,' he admitted with a wry smile. 'But I knew the instant I saw her that she was the one.'

'That does sound familiar! Where did you meet? How long have you known her?' his cousin queried, firing off questions.

'I met her in person on Monday, but we had been emailing for a month.'

'You are resorting to internet dating now?' Seb teased with a mischievous grin.

Irritated, Rico shook his head. 'Of course not.'

He explained the circumstances of their month-long correspondence, his plan to offer her a job, his reaction when he had seen her and his shock when he had found out who she was. 'She's the most amazing woman I've ever met. And she absorbs information like a sponge, Seb. She's so bright and skilled—and her care for her patients is second to none.'

A smile came unbidden as he relived the moment he had first set eyes on Ruth. Not only was she stunningly beautiful in a natural, understated way, but she was intelligent, interesting and intriguing, not to mention fun to be with. She aroused him as no other woman had ever done, yet her innate reserve, innocence and vulnerability brought out a protective side in him he had not known existed.

'It sounds like a cliché,' he continued, 'but our gazes met and it was as if my whole world changed in that split second. I had never felt like it before.'

Rico gave his cousin an edited version of what had happened during the two days that had followed. He remembered every second of his time with Ruth. Especially the passionate night they had shared. Ruth had been so unaware of her sexuality and shocked, at first, at the things they had done and the pleasure she had experienced. Coaxing out the inner vixen had been mind-blowing, and unlocking all that hidden, untapped passion intensely satisfying, not just in sexual terms but in knowing she had never felt it before. It made him want to beat his chest like some primitive caveman. She had blossomed, shedding her reserve and inhibitions, proving just how sensual and passionate she really was. And then she had slipped away like a thief in the night.

'I don't know why she ran—what it was that scared her,' he said, admitting his anxieties. 'I was so certain that she felt the same as me. Was I so wrong? And what am I going to do now?'

'Have you not spoken to her at all since Wednesday?' Seb asked, all hint of teasing now gone.

'No.' Rico wanted to growl his frustration. 'I still only have her email address—she could be anywhere in the UK. I begged her to at least let me know she had arrived home safely, and she did that much.' His fingers wrapped around the precious locket once more, his only tangible link with Ruth. 'I said I would give her a few days, if that was what she wanted, but no way am I going back to Italy without finding her, Seb. I can't let her go.'

'I thought you were anti-marriage…for yourself, at least.'

'No!' Seb's comment shocked him. 'Far from it. But I wasn't prepared to settle for anything less than what Mamma and Papà have. No woman has ever made me feel what Papà feels when he looks at Mamma. Or you, when you look at Gina. No woman has ever made me feel I could have that forever kind of love.'

Seb smiled. 'Until now.'

'Until now.' Again Rico dragged his fingers through his hair. 'I didn't think it would ever happen to me and then, when I least expected it, there she was.'

Moving the cats, Wallace and Sparky, from his lap to the adjacent sofa cushion, Seb stood up. 'It would be easy to trace her through the medical register. One moment. If Nic and Hannah do not have a copy, I can access it on my laptop.'

As his cousin left the room, Rico worried over Ruth's rejection. He had been so sure that she had been as lost in the magical connection between them as he had and he couldn't believe he had mis-judged her responses so completely. But Ruth *had* gone. He desperately needed to know why. And whether he still had a chance to win her round.

Seb arrived back, carrying a big red book. 'As I thought, Nic and Hannah had this copy on the bookshelves in their study. It's a year old—is that OK?' he asked, sitting down again, the cats immediately gravitating back to him.

'It should be. She said she had been in the practice for two years—although I don't think she is happy there.' He shook his head, despair tightening his gut. 'I learned so much about her in such a short time…her unhappy childhood, her shyness and reserve, her competence as a doctor but her complete lack of faith in herself as a woman. I thought we had crossed a bridge, that she trusted me, felt the same as me.' Rico paused a moment, steadying his voice. 'I can't walk away, Seb. I need her.'

His cousin watched him closely and nodded. 'Then we'll find her,' he stated confidently.

'I should not involve you in this. Tomorrow is your wedding day. I will look for her when you are away on your honeymoon,' Rico suggested, feeling guilty.

'Nonsense. I want to help. It would mean the world to me for you to be as happy as I am.' He opened the book and looked up expectantly. 'What is her name, *cugino*? Have you any clue where she comes from?'

'She is English, but I've no idea where she works. And her name is Ruth Baxter. She's so beautiful, Seb, with long, pale gold hair, amazing green eyes and a body to die for.'

Rico's heart swelled as he thought of the woman who had claimed his heart in such a short time, but his smile was tinged with sadness at having lost her so quickly. His confidence and belief had been shaken to the core, leaving him floundering for the first time in his life. The silence impinged on his consciousness and he realised that Seb was staring at him as if he had grown two heads.

'Seb?'

'Mio Dio!'

'What is the matter?' Rico asked with a frown. 'Why are you not looking in the book?'

Seb huffed out a breath. 'I do not need to look in the book,' he said, setting it aside.

'Why not? What are you doing?'

Confused, Rico watched as his cousin dislodged Wallace and Sparky from his lap once more, then twisted round to remove his wallet from the back pocket of his jeans. He drew something out and handed it over.

'Here.'

Rico rose to his feet and closed the distance between them. Several conflicting emotions rushed through him as he took the folded photograph Seb offered and found himself staring down at an image of Ruth. His whole body went rigid in surprise and confusion.

'Why do you have a picture of my woman?' he demanded, irritated when Seb laughed at him.

'Open it out, *cugino*.'

Rico did as he'd been told and saw the photograph was of three women. A pretty girl with wavy, honey-blonde hair and a shy smile. Gina, curvaceous, with dark hair and laughing dark eyes. And his Ruth, one of the group and yet exuding the air of aloneness that held her apart and tore at everything inside him.

'I don't understand,' he murmured, pressing the fingers of his free hand to his forehead.

'You will see your Ruth sooner than you expected, Rico.' Smiling, Seb rose to his feet and draped an arm around his shoulder. 'Ruth and Holly are Gina's best friends—and her two bridesmaids.'

Rico found himself back in the armchair, his legs too shaky to hold him. He sat in shock, unable to believe it. Ruth was in Strathlochan? Had been here all the time? He pressed a hand to his chest, feeling the rapid beat of his heart, trying to concentrate as Seb told him what he knew about Ruth. It matched up with what he had already discovered…her solitary life, her single-minded dedication to her career, her intelligence, her reserve.

'Even after eight months I don't know Ruth well, but I like her. I understand from Gina that she and Holly are the only real friends Ruth has ever had,' Seb finished, a reflective look on his face.

The coincidence that he and Seb should find love in the same place was extraordinary enough, but that it should turn out that Ruth should be here, too, was almost impossible to believe. Yet Ruth was in Strathlochan—and she was definitely the woman who had stolen his heart. Fate was telling him something. It was a sign. He and Ruth were meant to be. He knew it. Somehow he had to convince Ruth, too.

It was obvious now that he had miscalculated, Rico assessed. He had rushed Ruth earlier in the week and he would have to be careful not to do that again. He needed to get her to Florence and to win her agreement to take the job. Then he would have time to regain lost ground, to break through her insecurities and barriers, and to show her the kind of life they could have together, as equals and partners, friends and lovers, husband and wife.

'So, what are you going to do?'

Seb's question cut through his thoughts. 'Do?' He frowned, not sure what his cousin meant.

'Are you going to let Ruth know you are here?' Seb queried with a frown of his own. 'Or are you going to take her by surprise when she walks down the aisle tomorrow?'

Rico was not at all certain which was the best course of action. If Ruth found out now, would she run again? How would she feel if she came face to face with him in the church? Being so unsure of her and her feelings was playing havoc with his usual composure and rational decision-making.

'What do you think?' he asked his cousin.

'I think we tell Gina and see what she says,' Seb decided. 'I'll do everything I can to help you, Rico. I want you to be happy, and I'd be delighted if it was with Ruth. But I won't let anything spoil Gina's special day.'

Rico hid his frustration and nodded. 'I understand. Ring Gina.'

As Seb reached for his mobile phone, Rico's stomach was churning. Ruth was so close. He was desperate to see her, hold her, kiss her. But what if she told Gina that she didn't want to see him? What was he going to do then? All he knew was that he needed Ruth in his life and he would do whatever was necessary to earn her love.

CHAPTER EIGHT

HOLDING her mug in both hands, Gina leaned back on the sofa with a contented sigh. 'I won't believe the fairy tale is real until Seb and I are finally married. We seem to have been planning the wedding for ever, and at times I never thought the day would arrive. Now it's just hours away and I'm too buzzed and excited to sleep! I so hope nothing goes wrong. What if Seb doesn't turn up?' She bit her lip, momentary anxiety replacing the dreamy smile that was usually present on her face.

'Nothing is going to go wrong,' Ruth insisted firmly.

'And of course Seb is going to turn up!' Holly added with equal vehemence. 'He's madly in love with you.'

It was late on Friday night and Maria, Gina's grandmother, had long since gone to bed. Gina, Holly and herself should follow suit in preparation for an early start in the morning, Ruth admitted, but none of them had felt sleepy. Dressed in pyjamas, and savouring mugs of hot chocolate, they were curled on up one of the huge soft and squishy sofas in the living room of the large town house Seb had bought earlier in the year, Gina's tiny cottage proving too small and lacking privacy. Set back from the road, and secluded from its neighbours, the town house had a self-contained, ground-floor apartment for Maria, as well as a big garden and a priceless view of the loch and the hills rising behind it.

Their dog, Montgomery, was asleep in front of the log fire, his paws twitching as he chased rabbits in his dreams. The cosy atmosphere would never have affected her before, Ruth acknowledged, looking at her two friends with affection, emotion bringing a lump to her throat. Before… That was how everything was now divided. Before Rico and after Rico.

Being with him had breached some inner dam, cracking open the protective wall she had long used to shield herself from more hurt and rejection. Rico had taught her how to feel, and now she was exposed, with nothing to hide behind, and she was uncharacteristically emotional. She was also envious of Gina. Not that she begrudged her friend a single thing—Gina deserved all the happiness in the world. But the last few days had made Ruth realise how much was missing from her life and how desperately she wanted to be loved and cherished, too…by Rico.

The apparent hopelessness of *that* dream hit her anew. It had been a strain to keep up her front this evening, not to allow thoughts of Rico and her inner turmoil to burst free. With much of the talk being about Gina's sexy and devoted Italian husband-to-be, the contrasts were all too apparent, making her own situation hurt even more. It was a constant ache, gnawing away inside her. Closing her eyes, she sipped her drink, trying to shore up her shaky defences.

'I couldn't *think* of getting married without my two best friends beside me,' Gina said now, threatening Ruth's tenuous grasp on her self-control. 'I know neither of you like standing out in public, so it means even more that you said yes.'

'We only agreed when you promised there would be no hideous meringue-like dresses,' Ruth quipped, using humour to mask her feelings and making the others laugh.

She *had* been anxious about the dress, but she should have known better given Gina's person-ality and good taste. They'd had the final fittings back in April and she and Holly would be wearing the palest pink. Their sleeveless, knee-length dresses had scooped necklines and some same-colour beaded detail on the bodice. The cocktail-style dresses came with matching stoles that draped across their backs and came through their arms above the elbow, but could also be opened out and used as a wrap.

Gina's good taste had extended to her hen event, which had taken place two weeks ago. Instead of the raucous night out Ruth had feared, Gina had taken a handful of friends for a relaxing day being pampered at a spa, followed by a meal in the evening. Although she usually felt awkward and uncomfortable around people, Ruth had enjoyed the day…which said much about the kindness of Gina's circle of friends from within the local medical community, all of whom had embraced and included Ruth since her arrival in Strathlochan.

As well as Gina, Holly and herself, the hen group had included A and E registrar Annie Webster, who had made a full recovery from a frightening assault in Casualty in January and was now engaged to fellow trauma doctor Nathan Shepherd; hospital radiographer Francesca Scott, who had recently found love with her childhood hero when Luke Devlin, now an orthopaedic surgeon, had returned to Strathlochan after ten years away; former flight paramedic Callie McInnes, seven months pregnant and married to Frazer, a doctor on the local air ambulance; and Hannah Frost, a GP from the outlying village of Lochanrig, who was married to her Italian practice partner, Nic di Angelis.

Everyone around her was radiant with happiness and deeply in love, Ruth realised, a lump forming in her throat. Everyone but her. And Holly. Dear, sweet, gentle, caring Holly. Observing her friend, Ruth understood for the first time the sadness that dimmed Holly's outward smile and brought shadows to her sky-blue eyes. A nurse on the children's ward at Strathlochan Hospital, Holly was only interested in one man. But her relationship with A and E doctor Gus Buchanan had stalled before it had started, thanks to her scheming, manipulative older sister.

So Holly was alone…just like her. The hollow ache intensified inside her and Ruth leaned forward to set her empty mug on the coffee table, remaining there to keep herself hidden. How could she miss Rico so much? Where was he now? Did he think of her at all? Her whole life had changed the instant she had seen him and she felt out of her depth, uncertain, scared. A shiver rippled through her. When a gentle hand settled on her back, she tensed and sucked in a steadying breath.

'Ruth, honey, what's wrong?' Holly asked softly.

'Nothing.' Sandwiched between her two friends on the sofa, she sat up straight, trying to smile away the lie. 'I'm fine.'

Gina, curled up with her legs tucked beneath her, shook her head. 'You've been preoccupied this evening. And, although we've hardly seen you since you came back from that conference, there's something different about you. You have a new confidence, you hold your head up…your whole bearing is changed. We've both noticed it,' Gina added with alarming perception.

'I had a lot of work to cram into three days, especially as I'm off for the next two weeks dog-sitting Monty,' she excused herself, but the words sounded unconvincing even to her own ears.

Anxious, her fingers went out of habit to her locket, forgetting for a moment that it wasn't there. She plucked awkwardly at the neck of her top, but it was too late, Gina had noticed.

'Your locket!' her friend exclaimed, coming up on her knees and sliding an arm around Ruth's shoulder. 'Oh, Ruth, you haven't lost it, have you? I know how much it means to you. You *never* take it off—only for swimming.'

Ruth opened her mouth to try and explain away its absence, but her mind filled with memories of just why and how it had been removed. She recalled the way Rico had unfastened it, cradling it with care as he put it safely to one side. And then his touch had been for her alone. Goosebumps stood out on her skin, and it was almost as if she could still feel the caress of his fingers as he had soaped, teased and tormented her all over, could still see the hot appreciation in his gaze, and his sinfully wicked smile that had held the promise of what was to come. She shook her head, trying to banish the images and rush of emotion, but they overwhelmed her and a sob escaped unchecked.

Before she had the chance to escape and hide herself away, Gina and Holly closed in on either side of her and, as the tears she had tried so hard to keep at bay for days slid down her cheeks, they wrapped their arms around her.

'I'm sorry.' The apology emerged as a throaty murmur when the onslaught began to abate.

Ruth was aware of Gina stroking her hair, while Holly reached for the box of paper tissues on the nearby table, sitting back and handing some to her. 'Thanks.'

'What is it, Ruth?' Gina queried, and the sympathy and concern in her friend's voice nearly undid her all over again.

She shook her head, not wanting her insecurities and problems to worry Gina now of all times. 'I can't do this just before your wedding,' she protested.

'Nonsense! You matter to me, Ruth. To all of us,' Gina reassured her.

'I know it isn't easy for you to talk about things.' Holly, ever intuitive and understanding, took her hand. 'But we're your friends. We care. And we're always here for you. Please, let us help.'

Uncertain, Ruth shook her head again.

Gina's hold tightened, as if trying to share her strength. 'It's your mysterious specialist, isn't it? The one you've been emailing and met at the conference?'

'Yes,' Ruth admitted, shocked again at Gina's perception.

'What happened?' Holly asked, clearly worried. 'Did he hurt you?'

Ruth managed a teary laugh at the absurdity of that thought. 'No. Of course not.'

'He offered you a job—just as I feared he would,' Gina stated with pained resignation.

'Yes…but it's so much more than that. I—' Ruth stopped, unsure how to explain. Nibbling her lower lip, she looked from Holly to Gina. 'Is it possible to fall in love in two days?'

Her friends both gave exclamations of surprise, then Gina smiled. 'I did. I knew the moment I saw Seb that something unusual and special was happening.'

'Me, too,' Holly agreed, although her smile was tinged with such sadness that made Ruth want to cry again—that or knock some sense into Gus Buchanan.

'So he wasn't some avuncular, grandfather figure, then?' Gina teased, although concern remained evident in her dark brown eyes. 'Or the mad professor you pictured?'

Ruth's answering laugh was more genuine. 'Nothing remotely like that. The first time our gazes met, it was like an electric connection had been made, and I didn't even know who he was at that point…and he didn't know my identity, either. I've never experienced anything like it before,' she told them shyly.

'It must have been a surprise when you introduced yourselves!' Wide-eyed, Holly could hardly contain her eager curiosity. 'What happened then?'

To her amazement, Ruth found herself telling her friends the whole story. She had never revealed much about her past to them before, but now Gina and Holly were hanging on her every word as she spoke about her background, her parents, Adam, the conference, the accident at the restaurant—and Rico. His belief in her, the job offer, and how he had made her feel special and desired for the first time in her life.

'He told me that he wanted me, and he offered me a night out of time before reality and work intruded again the next day,' she confided, her cheeks flushing. 'I wanted him just as much. I wanted to know if Adam was wrong, and, just once, to see what it might be like with someone I responded to and cared about. Stupidly, I thought I could handle it.'

Tears threatened and Ruth paused, gaining comfort from her friends. 'It was the most incredible experience of my life. On Wednesday morning I knew that one night was never going to be enough. I wanted more…wanted him. But that wasn't in the rules.' Taking a deep breath, she lowered her gaze. 'I ran away. While he was still asleep. I know it was wrong—cowardly—but I couldn't face him, couldn't pretend that what we had shared meant nothing.'

'Oh, Ruth. Of course you are not a coward. It's understandable you felt as you did. And to think of all you've been through that we knew nothing about,' Gina finished, her own voice thick with emotion as she hugged her tight.

Holly squeezed her fingers. 'It must have been so difficult for you. Have you not heard from him since?'

'We hadn't yet exchanged other contact details—it didn't seem urgent at the time. I'm ashamed to say I went without leaving a note or anything. I was confused, scared and upset at finding him—feeling things I never believed I could—only to lose him again.' Ruth sighed, taking a ragged breath. 'He emailed and I felt so guilty as I'd clearly worried him. He begged me to at least let him know I was safe. I replied and said I needed to think. He answered, saying he would give me a few days if that's what I needed, that he had some business to take care of, but would contact me afterwards. And he found my locket. He's keeping it safe.' Ruth hesitated, not wanting to upset her friends. 'He still hopes I'll take the job.'

'And you want it.' Gina's statement rang with disappointment.

'More than anything, Gina. I've not felt this challenged and excited in a long time. But...' She shook her head, fighting indecision.

Holly's smile was kind and gentle. 'But you're worried about seeing him,' she stated with customary understanding.

'How could I work with him every day and be close to him, knowing I can't be *with* him? And can I trust my feelings? It's so sudden and I've had no experience. Is it really love? Or am I naively reacting to the first man who has made me feel wanted and who isn't intimidated by my brains?' she finished, expressing her worries aloud.

Gina's sigh was heartfelt. 'I want you to be happy, Ruth. And if this job calls to you, you should take it. Just as you should fight for this man if he is what you want. Not that I want you living in the United States,' she admitted with a watery smile.

'I wouldn't be,' Ruth corrected.

Holly voiced her surprise. 'I thought your mysterious doctor was American.'

'I did, too, but I was wrong,' Ruth explained. 'He was over there for consultations, lectures and so on, and he attended the conference on his way home.'

'So where *is* the job?' Gina asked, dark eyes showing a mix of relief and worry.

'Eventually, in the UK.' Ruth's enthusiasm and eager excitement bubbled through. 'But first I'll have to retrain and get some experience. He plans to open a new clinic in partnership with the NHS, and he suggested I could be part of that.'

'Where would you be living until then?' Holly asked.

'In Italy. His clinic is in Florence.'

Gina drew back with a startled 'Oh!' and a frown knotted her brow.

'What's wrong?' Puzzled, Ruth wondered why her friend sounded so odd.

'It's nothing,' Gina murmured, but she was pale, her gaze darting from Holly to Ruth and back again. 'You didn't tell us the name of this wonderful man.'

'Rico…Dr Riccardo Linardi,' she confided, surprised when Gina's cheeks flushed pink and she looked away.

'What does he look like?' Holly asked, diverting Ruth's attention. 'He's obviously a lot younger than we all thought.'

'He's thirty-four, and he's gorgeous. Seriously, heart-stoppingly beautiful, with a sexy bad-boy appeal. Not the kind of man you expect to meet in real life. When I first saw him, I thought he looked like a pirate!' Ruth felt warmth infuse her cheeks as she confided her uncharacteristically whimsical notions.

Both her friends laughed, but Gina's sounded more shrill than usual, and she was certainly no longer relaxed. Before Ruth could comment on Gina's odd behaviour and sudden restlessness, Holly was begging her to continue with her description of Rico. Whilst thinking about him was painful, Ruth found that sharing her feelings with her friends made the whole dream-like experience more real.

'He has dark hair, and it's longish—down to here.' Ruth used her hand to show where Rico's hair brushed over his collar to his shoulders. 'Several days' stubble add to the whole rakish rogue effect.' She closed her eyes for a moment, reliving the erotic and arousing sensation of his unshaven jaw caressing her sensitive skin. Oh, my! She cleared her throat and pulled herself together. 'His eyes are unusual…a dark hazel but with lots of gold flecks in them.'

'Wow! He sounds amazing,' Holly breathed.

Ruth crashed back to earth with a bump. 'He is. And I don't know what to do.'

'I think you should take the job.'

Gina's advice took Ruth by surprise. 'But you didn't want me to leave!'

'I don't.' Again her friend's smile seemed over-bright, and she fidgeted with her hands. 'I'll miss you like hell. But I know how things happened for me, and if you feel for Rico as I do for Seb, then you shouldn't throw away the chance for happiness.'

'Offering me the job doesn't mean Rico's interested in me personally. There's no guarantee he'll contact me again,' Ruth pointed out, fresh pain lancing through her.

'He will.'

Gina's about face and bold prediction took Ruth by surprise. She wished she had a fraction of her friend's confidence but even if Rico still wanted her to work for him, he had been clear enough about their one night together.

'I promised Seb I'd text him before I went to bed.' A furtive look in her eyes, Gina rose to her feet and fumbled on the table for her mobile phone. 'Damn! I'd forgotten I turned it off earlier.'

As Gina pressed the power button, they all

heard the rapid series of bleeps that notified she had numerous missed calls and text messages awaiting her.

'Last-minute wedding arrangements,' Holly guessed.

Gina shook her head, and Ruth saw her send Holly a speaking look, one Ruth couldn't decipher. 'I'll do this upstairs,' Gina announced, clutching the phone tightly.

'Are you OK?' Ruth asked, worried at the change in her friend's attitude.

'I'm all twitchy and excited. Don't mind me! Thank you for confiding in us, Ruth, it means a lot.' She paused, biting her lip. 'Your friendship means the world to me. More than anything I want you to be happy.'

Ruth's throat tightened with emotion. 'Thanks, Gina. I'm sorry to lay this on you the night before your wedding.'

'Don't apologise, please. I'm so glad and honoured you trusted us.' Gina hugged her again, then Holly. 'You're both brilliant. The best friends ever.'

'I think we should all get some sleep,' Holly suggested, rising to her feet and gathering up the empty mugs. 'I'll wash these up.'

Gina called Monty. The dog stretched his

lanky limbs and got to his feet, his tail wagging enthusiastically as he trotted to her side. Ruth helped Gina make the fire safe, then double-checked that the doors were locked, by which time Holly had caught up with them. They went upstairs together. After another round of good-nights, Ruth found herself alone in one of the welcoming guest bedrooms.

As she snuggled under the duvet, her mind refused to switch off. Something had happened to change Gina's mood, but Ruth couldn't put her finger on what it was. She hoped there had been no upsetting news amongst the unusually large number of messages waiting on Gina's phone. Nothing could happen to spoil the wedding day.

Being able to share her emotions and worries with her friends was a new experience, and she did feel better for it—even if she remained at a loss to know what to do about Rico. A nagging voice insisted that the magic couldn't be real and nothing more was going to come of it. But her time with Rico had been so intense, so incredible. She wanted everything they had been together to mean something more to him than a one-night stand. And she wanted more of Rico…something he was unable to give.

There was nothing else she could do tonight, Ruth reasoned, turning out the light. Tomorrow she would try to hide her own worries and make sure that Gina's special day was perfect as she married the man she loved—a man who, with every look and word and gesture, demonstrated that he so clearly loved Gina in return. A fresh pang of envy pierced Ruth's heart. If only Rico felt that way about her.

She would get through tomorrow. She *would*. And afterwards there would be time to make decisions about her career and the rest of her life. If Rico *did* contact her again, she knew she couldn't lose the greatest job opportunity she would ever have because she had a crush on him. More than a crush. But she was an adult. A professional. She would deal with it and take whatever chances came her way.

And, somehow, some day, the hurt would begin to ease and she would get over Rico… wouldn't she?

'Are you ready to go, *cugino*?'

Rico drained the last of his coffee, rinsed the mug and set it on the drainer in Nic and Hannah's kitchen. 'I am ready.'

'To look at you, all anxious and shaky, anyone

would think *you* were the one getting married,' Seb teased as he led the way outside to the car.

'I wish I was.'

Seb draped an arm around his shoulders. 'All being well, it soon will be. You are really so worried?'

'I have no idea how Ruth will react,' Rico admitted, slipping into the passenger seat and fastening the seat belt as Seb took his place behind the wheel. Nic and Hannah—who had been briefed about Ruth and sworn to secrecy— had gone on ahead. 'Any confidence I had about her feelings for me disappeared when she sneaked away on Wednesday morning.'

With a sigh, Rico turned his head and looked out of the window at the passing scenery as Seb took the rural roads from Lochanrig to the county town of Strathlochan. He was more than nervous. After the lengthy discussions late last night when Gina had finally turned on her phone and responded to Seb's pleas to call him, Rico was even more uncertain and anxious. It seemed Ruth had confided in Gina at about the same time that he had confessed his feelings to Seb.

Having made up his mind that he did not want Ruth to feel as if she had been tricked or deceived and that she should be told, Gina had decreed otherwise, anxious lest Ruth stayed away from the wedding. With Seb understanding his plight but supporting Gina's wishes, Rico had had little option but to go along with them, but he remained uneasy at the decision. It also bothered him that Gina believed Ruth would try to avoid him. What had Ruth said to her friends? He thought back to what Gina had said on the phone last night.

'Thank you for all you have done for Ruth.'

'How do you mean?' he had asked, puzzled by Gina's words.

'Even in a week she has changed. Holly and I knew very little about her background or her past, and we never liked to push because she was so reserved about it. Tonight, for the first time ever, Ruth confided in us and told us the real story of her parents, her upbringing, her bastard of a boyfriend,' Gina had explained, her voice thick with unshed tears. 'You've clearly touched something in her, changed her, but she's on new ground, Rico, and she's confused and scared.'

He had dragged his fingers through his hair in agitation. 'I know, Gina. I misjudged things and rushed Ruth. I don't plan to make that mistake again,' he had reassured her, explaining his fledgling plan to persuade Ruth to visit

Florence, to keep things focused on work and then to slowly rebuild their relationship.

'I think that's a good idea. I hate the thought of Ruth going away, but I want her to be happy. I know she wants the job…and I think you will be good together. I'll do what I can to help.'

Ruth wanted the job—but did she want him? The question occupied his mind for the duration of the journey, until Seb turned the car in at the gateway of Strathlochan Castle—manned for the day by a security team to keep out the uninvited—and drove round the impressive building to park near the small chapel where the ceremony was to take place. Rico climbed out of the car and took a deep breath of clear Scottish air. He allowed his gaze to sweep over the granite edifice of the castle buildings, set in gardens ablaze with the vibrant blooms of rhododendrons and azaleas, then across the shimmering blue waters of the loch to the woods and hills beyond.

It made an impressive setting for what Seb and Gina had chosen to be a small and discreet occasion. Or as discreet as an Adriani/Linardi occasion ever could be, Rico amended, noting the presence of the invited media with distaste. Seb, wanting everything perfect for his lovely bride, had done a deal with a local newspaper and a respected Italian magazine, offering exclusive pictures on the understanding that no word leaked out to turn the wedding into a circus.

With his own parents attending—his father, Robert, a wealthy corporate attorney and his mother, Sofia, widely recognised for her tireless charity campaigns and work with UNICEF—there was bound to be interest from the press. And, despite the change in his circumstances following injuries sustained last summer which prevented his return to the operating room, Seb's former status as a famous reconstructive plastic surgeon to the stars meant interest in him had not yet faded.

'I hope your agreement has been honoured,' Rico murmured as they walked towards the entrance to the private chapel.

Seb nodded, a guarded expression on his face as the two photographers recorded his arrival. 'I had forgotten how tedious the whole paparazzi thing was. It's one of the many advantages of living here. I think they know it is more than their lives are worth to break the contract. Not only would they lose the kudos of their story, but Zio Roberto would come down on them for all he was worth.'

'That is true.'

Smiling, he followed Seb into the church, delighted to find his parents waiting to greet them. He had not seen them since he had left for the United States and he embraced them both warmly. Unfortunately, there was no time to brief them about Ruth, but he looked forward to introducing them at the reception. For now he had his duty to do. In front of the altar, he checked his pocket for the umpteenth time to confirm the rings were safe, then surreptitiously glanced at his watch, hoping that Gina was not going to keep them waiting too long.

Rico looked up, frowning when he discovered Seb, Nic and Hannah watching him with equal parts of amusement and sympathy. Hell, he thought, shifting from foot to foot in agitation, his cousin was right. He was far more nervous than the groom! If only he could be as certain of Ruth as Seb was of Gina. His gut tightened and his heart started beating in a crazy rhythm when whispers from the entrance of the chapel announced that the bridal car was in sight. After four long days of missing her, he would see his Ruth any moment now. The thought of what might happen then made him sick with nerves…Ruth held his heart, his life, his whole future, in the palms of her hands.

* * *

'We're here!' Holly announced with excitement as the luxury car paused at the castle gate to clear the security check and then proceeded serenely up the drive.

'As long as Seb is here,' Gina responded, her smile betraying her nerves.

Ruth sat forward and looked out of the window, unsurprised but wary when she saw the four members of the press who had been granted conditional access make a move towards the car, ready to snap the first pictures of the bride. She knew Gina had been relieved that Seb had managed to keep things as quiet as possible. Her gaze moved on. Callie and Frazer waited at the door of the chapel—the venue of their own Christmas Eve marriage ceremony five months before and now host to Gina and Seb's. Callie grinned, giving a thumbs-up signal, and Ruth smiled.

'Seb's here,' she reassured her friend. 'Not that there was any question of it.' Ruth winked at Maria and Holly. 'Unless you're having doubts, Gina. You don't have to go through with it if you don't want to.'

'Not go through with it? Are you crazy? I can't *wait* to marry Seb!'

Ruth joined in with the collective laughter as

Gina rose indignantly to the bait, but she could not brush off the unease she had been feeling all morning. They had made an early start, but she had been the last one down for breakfast, and when she had pushed open the kitchen door, a hush had fallen in the room. Gina, Holly and Maria had worn identical expressions of guilt and uncertainty.

In the hectic few hours that had followed, several strange things had happened, but Ruth had been too busy to assess them or to ask questions of the three women who kept darting looks at her. The hairdresser had been to style their hair, and excitement had built until the time had come for them all to get dressed. Holly, who had happily assigned herself the task of watching over Maria for the day, had gone to help the elderly lady with her outfit, while Ruth had remained to help Gina.

In a departure from tradition, Gina had chosen a unique design for her wedding dress, declaring herself unsuited to trains, frills, lace and acres of petticoats and veils. The apparently simple style of the halter-neck dress was deceptive. The ivory colour accentuated the warm tones of Gina's skin, while the silken fabric had been designed to show off her womanly curves to perfection.

The front was ruched from breast to thigh and had a river of glittering silvery beads flowing down in a narrow, wavy line to one hip. At the back, there was a V-shaped panel with eyes through which ran the satin ribbon that acted like the stays on an antique bodice and laced the dress together. Careful not to draw it in too tight, Ruth had fastened the ribbon in a bow at the small of Gina's back. The same style of beadwork used on the front decorated either side of the panel on the back. The skirt was cut at an angle, finishing mid-thigh on one side and just below the knee on the other.

As the car came to a halt, Ruth climbed out one side and Holly the other, and they waited to help their charges. As Holly aided Maria, Ruth held Gina's bouquet of cream and pink sweet peas, the same flowers that had been woven into Gina's long ebony hair.

'You look absolutely stunning,' Ruth told her friend as they walked towards the ornately carved wooden doors that stood open to welcome them. 'Seb is going to take one look and want to eat you alive!'

Radiant with happiness and eager anticipation, Gina grinned. 'I do hope so!'

They reluctantly posed for a few photographs, then stepped inside the cool and atmospheric old chapel. For a moment they paused to make a few last-minute adjustments to their clothing, and again Ruth noticed the anxious look that passed between Gina, Holly and Maria.

'You are ready, *ragazza mia*?' Maria asked, tears shimmering in her eyes.

Gina nodded, giving Holly a hug. Ruth thought she heard Gina whisper 'Look out for her', but she couldn't be sure, although she imagined the instruction concerned Maria. Then Gina turned and Ruth found herself enveloped in a hug, too.

'Forgive me. I love you and want you to be happy,' her friend murmured in her ear. 'I'm ready, Nonna.'

Frowning as Gina pulled away, Ruth opened her mouth to ask what she meant, but her words were drowned as the organist struck the opening bar of the music chosen for the bride's entrance. Maria patted her arm, then, side by side, and as Gina's only living relative, grandmother and granddaughter began their journey towards the altar.

A shiver of disquiet rippled down Ruth's spine as she fell into step with Holly. What was she missing? The question nagged at her as she followed Gina and Maria. For a moment Ruth's stride faltered as she experienced again that inexplicable feeling of being watched. She glanced around the small chapel that was full of invited friends, almost all from Strathlochan's various medical services, but no one seemed to be paying her undue attention, all of them focused on the beautiful bride.

Ruth could not shake off the strange sensation as she continued down the aisle. As they neared the front, she caught a glimpse of Seb, whose expression of pride, love and sensual promise as he looked at Gina was just as Ruth had imagined it would be. It brought an ache to her heart and a hopeless wish that this might one day happen to her.

Maria, tearful but happy, placed Gina's hand in Seb's and moved aside. Ruth took her place next to Holly, puzzled when her friend shifted closer, then reached for her fingers and gave them a squeeze.

'What?' Ruth mouthed silently, but Holly just shook her head.

The priest cleared his throat and a reverent hush descended in the chapel. Seb and Gina stepped forward to take their place in front of the altar. The action brought Seb's cousin, who was acting as his best man, into view for the first time. Wearing a charcoal suit, crisp white shirt and a silver-blue silk tie, he looked as if he had stepped from the pages of *Vogue*. Ruth's breath lodged in her throat and she experienced an overwhelming sense of *déjà vu* as her gaze roved upwards and clashed with his. As soon as she had begun the walk down the aisle she'd had the unsettling feeling that she was being watched. Now she knew why. Waves of emotion crashed through her.

Dear God! Ruth's heart skipped several beats and she nearly fainted in shock as she discovered what—or *who*—her friends had been keeping from her. She was dimly aware of them watching her now, but Ruth couldn't move or say a word.

All she could do was stare in helpless disbelief into Rico's sultry gold-flecked hazel eyes.

CHAPTER NINE

'MAMMA, Papà, I want you to meet Ruth
Baxter...one of Gina's best friends and a very
gifted doctor.'

With his hand resting on the curve of her hip,
Rico drew Ruth forward as he made the intro-
ductions. He felt protective and proprietorial,
and, having missed her terribly these last few
days, he was determined not to let Ruth out of
his sight. The moment she had walked down the
aisle behind Seb and Gina, Rico had been impa-
tient to go to her. She had looked hauntingly
beautiful. And whilst he had noticed a change in
the way she carried herself, as if she was less
self-conscious, he had seen at once the vulnerability that remained in her sage-green eyes.

Some people were intimidated by her beauty
and intelligence, but intimidated was not at all
how Rico felt around Ruth. Stimulated, yes.
Charged. Challenged. Impressed. From the
second he had seen her again, every atom of his

being had surged with excitement and arousal, proving that his feelings were real and not a fantasy. Ruth was *the one*. He looked at her now, noting how the pale pink dress suited her to perfection, the cut highlighting her slender figure, the pale pink bringing a warm glow to her alabaster skin. She was natural, elegant and graceful…and she took his breath away.

Ruth was yet to recover from her shock at seeing him, Rico knew, and he had not been able to engineer even the shortest time alone with her to explain. From the moment the wedding ceremony had ended, he had been by her side, his arm around her to support, to guard and to stake his claim. He was aware of her discomfort—which he hoped was due to her unease at being in a crowd and not because of him.

With the obligatory photographs having been taken outside the chapel, everyone had relocated to the castle's function room where the reception was being held. Before taking their assigned places for the lunch, Rico had managed to draw Ruth aside, anxious for her to meet the other people who had a special place in his life.

Although convinced his parents would love Ruth, he felt a sense of anticipation now that the moment had arrived. He had not been able to brief them, so he switched to Italian to hide from Ruth the meaning of his words.

'La donna che ho intenzione di sposare.'

His declaration of intent to marry Ruth was met by puzzled incomprehension from the lady herself—Rico sighed with relief that his gamble had paid off and she had not understood—and with the open delight he had expected from his parents. As they greeted her with warmth and enthusiasm, he kept Ruth close to his side, breathing in her subtle but arousing lavender scent.

'Ruth, it is so lovely to meet you, *mia cara.*' Smiling, and exuding the customary charm so familiar to him, his mother embraced Ruth. 'I know we shall be very good friends and I will look forward to spending time with you.'

'Thank you, Signora Linardi,' Ruth murmured, her answering smile shy.

'Please, you must call me Sofia.'

His father eagerly shook the hand Ruth offered to him. 'And I am Roberto, my dear,' he greeted, kissing her on both cheeks.

'I am trying to persuade Ruth to come and work at the clinic,' Rico explained, feeling the quiver that shimmered through her. 'She has a brilliant mind and a caring heart. One day I hope she will help me open the new clinic in the UK.'

'That would be wonderful,' his father responded with infectious enthusiasm.

His mother nodded in agreement. 'We will look forward to welcoming you to Florence very soon, Ruth.'

'That's kind, thank you. But nothing has been decided yet.'

Ruth's words demonstrated how much work he still needed to do. And, however difficult—when all he wanted to do was to take her in his arms and make love to her—he had to remember his vow that, if given a second chance, he would take things more slowly. Anxious not to pressure her, Rico reluctantly eased back.

'I think it is time we took our places for the meal,' he suggested, drawing attention to the fact that the guests were now seated.

'Of course.' His mother smiled and rested the palm of one hand against Ruth's cheek. 'I hope we will have more time to talk today, *mia cara*, before Roberto and I must leave. Unfortunately this is just a flying visit for us as I have an important function to attend in London for UNICEF. But nothing could keep us away from seeing Seb and Gina marry! And it is good to see Nic and Hannah again.'

They parted company, his parents joining Nic

and Hannah at the table nearest to the bride and groom's party. Rico escorted Ruth to the main table, grateful that Seb, Gina, Holly and Maria had arranged things so that he and Ruth would be side by side. Hating to lose the physical contact even for a moment, Rico released Ruth and held out her chair, waiting for her to settle before he sat down.

The arrival of the waiters with the first course delayed conversation, and Rico slid his hand into his jacket pocket, his fingers closing around Ruth's locket. He would wait until they had a quiet moment alone before fixing it back in place around her slender neck.

'What did your mother mean about Nic and Hannah?' Ruth's softly voiced question drew him from his thoughts.

'It is another strange coincidence—there must be something in the Strathlochan air!' he joked. 'I did some of my medical training at a hospital in Milan. Nic was working there for a short time and we became friends. He visited us in Florence a few times, and I came to Lochanrig when he and Hannah married. It was a big surprise when Seb discovered the connection between Gina, Strathlochan and Nic,' he added, explaining how that had come about.

'I had no idea.' Ruth shook her head, pausing a moment before continuing. 'Your mother mentioned UNICEF?'

Thankful that she was beginning to relax a little, Rico ignored his starter and gave Ruth his full attention, noting that their table companions were engrossed in a discussion of their own—a thoughtful if unsubtle attempt to give him time with Ruth.

'Mamma has devoted herself to charity work for as long as I can remember.' He leaned closer, taking care not to crowd her. 'She did much for local groups in Florence, which won her recognition and appeals for help, support and advice from national and international organisations. For the last decade or so she has been involved with UNICEF and has visited many regions where children are in great need, heading campaigns and working tirelessly to raise funds and awareness.' Pausing to take a sip of his wine, he indulged his desire to look at Ruth. 'I am sure Mamma would love to talk with you about it.'

'I'd be very interested to hear of her work. And your father?'

Rico followed Ruth's gaze to the nearby table where his parents were laughing with Nic, Hannah and a couple of other guests he did not know. 'Papà is an attorney. He is in private practice and he specialises in corporate law, advising individual firms on issues from compliance and tax to employment issues and mergers. He also works with prosecuting authorities in various cases including fraud, financial crime, patent infringement, counterfeit goods, workers' rights, corporate environmental abuses...that kind of thing.'

'Environmental abuses like toxic chemical leaks?' Ruth queried, an endearing knot of concentration creasing her brow.

'Thankfully cases are rarely on a devastating scale,' he told her, 'but, yes, pollution or degradation of the environment that impacts on people's lives.'

'You sound very proud of them—and I'm not surprised. Your parents are lovely.'

The wistful edge to her voice broke his heart. His arm rested along the back of her chair, and now he slid his fingers under the silken fall of her hair, finding her muscles knotted with tension. Out of sight of everyone else, he began a gentle massage, the only physical comfort he could offer given the setting they were in.

Green eyes, filled with shadows and confusion, stared into his. A sigh whispered from her and Rico felt her easing under his touch, some of the tension draining away as she relaxed into him. He hated it that Ruth had not known the same love and support that he had enjoyed growing up, and he wanted to make everything better. Although he could not change the past, he would do all he could to ensure her future was a happy one. If she let him. His parents would welcome her to the family and treat her as the daughter they'd never had. Their warmth and love was a gift he could give her. But first he had to regain her trust...and win her heart.

Their starter plates were taken away and the main course of salmon arrived. Rico reluctantly withdrew his hand from Ruth, his mind preoccupied as he ate. Her life experiences had been so different from his own. As a child he'd had security, love and an example of an excellent marriage—so much so he had determined never to settle for less. Ruth had only known parents who had been cold and uncaring...to her and to each other.

Rico understood Ruth's confusion. He had ever experienced anything like this before and it was taking some getting used to...and that was with the positive example of his parents to follow. Ruth had none of that. Not only had she missed out on love as a child, but her excuse of a boyfriend had shredded and destroyed any fragments of self-confidence she'd had left. Whilst he may have accepted straight away that Ruth was the one for him, he could not expect her to have had such surety from day one. *He* was certain, but even he knew they were obstacles to overcome, so it must be much scarier and more confusing for her.

Ruth's insecurities had deep roots and were not going to be overcome at once. He had rushed her the first time. Now he had to move carefully if he hoped to turn the dream of having Ruth by his side for ever…his equal, his friend, his lover…into a reality. It would not be easy, but he hoped to keep the focus on work to begin with and to persuade Ruth to accompany him to Florence. Then, slowly, they could get their personal relationship back on track. One thing was certain—no way was he going to let Ruth slip away. She touched something deep within him, filling an empty space he had never known existed until he had met her. He needed her. And for the first time in his life, something, some*one*, was more important than his work.

A burst of applause startled Rico from his introspection, and he looked up in time to see Seb and Gina rise and prepare to cut the cake. Rico reached for Ruth's hand under the table and linked their fingers, needing the contact. The next few hours would be crucial as he put the first stage of his plan into action. There was no room for error. Or failure. Not if he hoped to succeed in achieving the two things he wanted most. Ruth working with him…and marrying him.

Ruth felt as if she was on an emotional rollercoaster. The wedding ceremony had passed in a blur and now, the meal over and the cake having been cut, she sat at her place at the bride and groom's table as Seb, Maria and Rico took it in turns to make their speeches. She felt strange…as if she was watching everything unfold in front of her like scenes from a film, with her on the outside looking in. It wasn't real. And yet it was.

She would never forget the moment her gaze had clashed with Rico's in front of the chapel's altar, or the moment the truth had dawned—that he was Seb's cousin. How long had he known? Why had no one said anything? Because it had been clear that they knew. Besides Rico, Gina, Seb, Holly, Maria, Nic and Hannah had all watched her with a mix of interest, anxiety and guilt. Why had they deceived her? Were they all laughing at her?

It was as if the foundations had been knocked from beneath her. And it was Rico, the cause of her shock, who had become her anchor. The width of the aisle had separated them, yet his gaze had felt like a physical touch, exciting and calming her at one and the same time. She had not been able to look away from him. Her heart had been thudding, her breathing shallow, and the ache of want, which had become familiar since she had met him less than a week ago, had tightened deep inside her.

The only part of the service that had impinged on her consciousness had come when Seb and Gina had exchanged their vows. Locked gaze to gaze with Rico, it had been an impossibly intimate moment. Ruth had felt the tug, the electric charge, the emotional pull, as if they were silently exchanging vows of their own.

Attentive and protective, Rico had been by her side since they had left the chapel. She had been nervous meeting his parents, but Sofia and Roberto Linardi had been warm and friendly. The smart of envy hit her once more. How she wished she'd had parents like them. During the meal—and she had no idea what she had eaten—she had been expecting questions and recriminations about the way she had left him at the hotel, but Rico had not said a word about it. Maybe their night together had not meant anything to him after all. She had to prepare herself for that.

He squeezed her fingers, and she looked up, meeting that enigmatic hazel gaze. She wanted to drink in every detail, to be as close to him as possible, and yet she was wary, uncertain, her defences in tatters. When he released her and rose to his feet to give his speech, Ruth missed his touch. She clenched her hands into fists in her lap. Despite her confusion, her indecision about what to do, her sole focus remained on Rico as he made everyone laugh with his stories about Seb.

His impact on her was as great now as when she had first seen him on Monday. At some point since she had left him, he had shaved, but already the roguish pirate stubble was growing back to shadow his masculine jaw. It was not a look she had found appealing before. But this was Rico…and in her eyes it suited him to perfection.

Before she knew it, the formalities were over and Seb whisked Gina off to the dance floor. As other guests began to join them, Rico stood up and held out his hand to her. Ruth didn't hesitate. She loved dancing but rarely had the chance. Now it gave her an excuse to be held in his arms once more, and she didn't know how many more opportunities she might have to be there. Trembling with excitement—and nerves—she placed her hand in his, feeling the jolt as the physical connection was made.

Leaving Holly and Maria chatting at the table as they indulged in a second slice of the sinfully delicious white chocolate and strawberry wedding cake, Ruth allowed Rico to lead her to the floor and draw her into his arms. It was heaven to be held by him again. Ruth closed her eyes, inhaling his warm and familiar cedar-wood scent. She wished she had the courage to press herself against him, but Rico was holding her chastely and she was too uncertain—of herself and of him—to make any kind of move. She didn't want to make even more of a fool of herself, especially if Rico *was* to be her boss and nothing more.

'Gina looks so beautiful, doesn't she?' Ruth asked, smiling as Seb spun his laughing bride around.

'She looks lovely,' Rico agreed, watching the

couple for a moment longer before his gaze returned to her, the expression in his eyes sultry and intense. 'But not as beautiful as you.'

A flush warmed her cheeks and she felt as tongue-tied as a teenager in the presence of her first crush rather than a professional adult. But Rico had that affect on her—and she'd had so little experience of men that she was unsure how to handle Rico or her responses.

'You and Seb seem very close,' she ventured after a moment, deciding it was safer to keep to neutral topics.

'We are.' Rico's breath fanned her cheek and a shiver rippled through her. 'Have Seb or Gina not told you how he came to live with us?'

Ruth shook her head. 'I only know that he stayed with his aunt and uncle—your parents,' she added, still struggling to absorb the coincidence.

'That is so, but there is much more to it.'

As they moved together in a slow waltz, Ruth listened in surprise as Rico explained the story.

'Seb's father was Mamma's brother. He died suddenly of a ruptured aortic aneurysm when Seb was eight, and his mother, unbalanced and involved with drugs, took Seb and disappeared. My parents never gave up searching for them, but it was three years before Seb was found… living by his wits on the streets after his mother had died some months before,' he told her, the tone of his voice betraying his emotions.

'That's awful.' Appalled, her gaze strayed to where Seb and Gina were dancing, clearly lost in each other. 'What happened?'

'I am sure there is much about Seb's life at that time that I do not know about even to this day, and I can only imagine what he went through,' Rico continued, his hand at her back urging her closer. 'Seb was found on the street, very ill with food poisoning. He was eleven then. The nuns who took him in remembered the notices and posters about a lost boy and contacted Papà.'

Ruth's attention was caught as Rico went on to describe the wild and untrusting boy who had been taken to live at the Linardis' home in Florence, and how a bond had formed between Seb and Rico. With only three months separating them in age, they had become as close as could be, and that friendship had endured into adulthood, both of them going to medical school until they had finally parted as their chosen specialties had taken them in different directions.

'We have been more brothers than cousins. The injuries Seb sustained going to the aid of a stranger being mugged last summer left him no longer able to operate,' he told her, touching on the part of Seb's story that Ruth knew. 'He was devastated. Surgery had been his life. I offered him a place at the clinic, but immunology and allergy never interested him. He was at a low point when he went to the villa on Elba to convalesce…and then he met Gina and his life changed.' A smile, tinged with something she could not decipher, crossed his face as he looked at Seb and Gina. 'I looked around the drop-in clinic on Thursday and met Thornton Gallagher. Right away I could see why Seb feels so right there. I'm delighted he is happy—and that he has found love—but I miss seeing him as much as I used to. So much has happened since we were eleven-year-old playmates.'

'I can imagine you both as naughty little boys and partners in crime,' Ruth admitted, smiling at the mental picture of him and Seb in their youth, touched by his words and the unexpected vulnerability he'd made no effort to hide.

'You are mistaken.' Rico's mock indignation was offset by the twinkle of answering amusement in gold-speckled hazel eyes. 'I was an angelic child.'

Ruth couldn't contain her laughter. 'I'm sure

your mother would tell me differently,' she teased, glancing across at Sofia Linardi who was now dancing with Seb while Roberto partnered Gina.

'It is good to hear you laughing again, *sirena mia*.'

The endearment, and the low, sexy timbre of Rico's accented voice, tightened the ache of longing inside her and brought a lump to her throat. Laughter fading, her gaze returned to his, her breath catching at the intimate expression in his eyes. His hand released hers and moved to cup her face. Her skin tingled from the brush of his fingers and she instinctively sought his touch, pressing her cheek into the warmth of his palm. Confusion reigned within her. Her mind was at war with the needs of her body, and her heart was stuck in between.

'Rico—' She fell silent as the pad of his thumb softly stroked the swell of her lips.

'Come with me.'

Weak-willed, she offered no resistance as he guided them to the edge of the busy dance floor and out of the door into a side room where they were alone. Before she could gather her scattered wits, Rico released her, slipping one hand into the pocket of his jacket and withdrawing her locket.

'Hold your hair up for me, *carissima*,' he instructed softly.

Ruth did as he requested, gathering up the loose strands of her hair, expecting Rico to move behind her. Instead, he stepped closer still. She felt the warmth of his body millimetres from her own and breathed in his scent as he bent his head and reached round to fasten the chain's clasp at the back of her neck. His fingers brushed tantalisingly against her skin as they completed their task and then whispered back along her neck and throat. Awareness had her pulse racing as his fingers skimmed on down the length of the chain to the upper swell of her breasts. There, he cradled the intricately engraved platinum locket. Ruth tried not to breathe as each rise and fall brought her skin into contact with his.

'Now it is back in its rightful place.'

'Thank you for looking after it.' Her voice was unsteady, her whole being attuned to his. 'It belonged to my grandmother. She was the only one who had time for me,' she found herself telling him. 'She died when I was nine. It's all I have left of her.'

Rico's arm came around her once more, a ragged breath escaping him. *'Sirena mia...'*

Whatever he had been going to say was fore-stalled when a knock sounded and the door opened a few seconds later. Gina and Seb came into the room, apologetic smiles on their faces.

'Can I borrow Ruth for a few minutes?' Gina asked.

'Of course.' Rico's agreement was polite, but Ruth sensed his reluctance as he slowly withdrew his arm. 'I will wait outside with Seb.'

Gina's smile was tremulous. 'Thanks.' She gave Rico a quick hug as he passed her, then waited until the door had closed before closing the gab between them. 'Hi,' she whispered. 'Are you still speaking to me?'

Seeing how genuinely upset her friend was, Ruth nodded. 'The shock is wearing off.' Her own attempt at a smile faded. 'How long have you known?' she asked, a flicker of hurt remaining that everyone had somehow been laughing at her.

'I had no idea until you mentioned Rico's name last night. That's why I was acting strangely. I was stunned. And I didn't know what to do, so I didn't immediately say anything,' she confessed, and Ruth knew at once that she was telling the truth. 'Seb had the same revelation from Rico at much the same time, hence all those messages on my mobile phone. They were all from Seb. He and Rico were as shocked at the coincidence as I was. Rico had no idea you were based in Strathlochan, or that you were going to be a bridesmaid at our wedding, where he would also be best man!'

'What did Rico say?' Ruth hated asking, but she couldn't stop herself.

'He'd been telling Seb how you had been in contact discussing your patient, how meeting you had completely floored him, and that he'd been upset when you left as you did,' Gina added, making Ruth feel bad all over again. 'I know how much he respects you and wants you on his team. He said he was giving you the space you wanted, but he planned to track you down after the wedding. Seb suggested looking in the medical register and that's when Rico told Seb your name. Seb showed Rico your photo—the one he took of you, Holly and me at Easter. Rico all but keeled over when he realised you were already here!'

Ruth thought over what Gina had said. She still didn't know if Rico was interested in her for herself, or if this was only about the job.

'Looking back, I don't know why it never occurred to me before, why I never put two and two together long ago,' Gina continued, her characteristic bubbly enthusiasm returning. 'But last night was the first time you told us Rico's name. And that he was from Florence. Until then I assumed the specialist you were emailing was American. My mind has been so full of the wedding, I've not focused on anything else.'

'You couldn't have guessed. What I don't understand is why you kept it from me today. You all seemed to know. Was that Rico's doing?' Ruth asked, nerves making her feel queasy.

Gina shook her head vehemently. 'No! Please, Ruth, don't blame Rico. It's my fault, not his. When I talked to Seb last night, he asked what I wanted to do. Rico wanted to warn you, so that you wouldn't feel tricked, but…'

'But?' Ruth prompted, her initial hurt dissipating with the knowledge that she had not been made fun of…and that it was not Rico who had deceived her.

'I'm sorry, Ruth. I asked them not to tell you. For two reasons.' Gina explained, bit her lip as she paused. 'I know you ran from Rico on Wednesday and I was scared you might do it again if you knew he was here. Selfishly, I wanted and needed you to be part of the wedding.'

'I would never have missed celebrating this day with you.' Ruth hoped that was as true as she wanted it to be and that she would not have panicked at the last minute. She was glad she had not been tested. 'And the other reason?'

Gina took her hand, her expression earnest. 'You've been different since you met Rico—even before you physically saw him and were just exchanging emails there was a change in you. I know you've always said you are not interested in men—and now I understand why. But with the right person, it is so amazing, Ruth. I would give anything for you to be as happy and fulfilled with Rico as I am with Seb.'

'I don't know, Gina. Everything has become so confused and mixed up with the job,' she admitted, trying to explain her muddled thoughts.

'I understand if you think I have interfered enough.' Gina hesitated, indecision evident in her dark eyes. 'May I offer some advice?'

Ruth nodded, knowing she could trust her friend.

'I think you should go to Florence. You aren't happy at the practice here, and you light up when you talk about the job with Rico. It would be perfect for you.' She gave a sad smile. 'I'd miss you like hell, but I wouldn't have a second's hesitation in entrusting you to Rico. Go…find out if the job is really what you want. Take it if it is. And then,' she added with a mischievous smile, 'if you want Rico, too, go and get him. Don't throw it all away, Ruth, because you are scared. The end result is so worth it. I think you need Rico—and I think Rico needs you.'

Emotion clogged Ruth's throat. She didn't know what to say. 'What if Rico only wants me to work for him? What if my feelings aren't real and I just reacted to the first man who was kind to me? How do I know?' The questions slipped out before she could stop them, revealing her inner vulnerability.

'Only you can find the answers.' Again Gina hesitated, looking unsure, but she shook her head and continued. 'Take things slowly. Go to Florence. You have the next two weeks off work—'

'To dog-sit Monty while you are on your honeymoon,' Ruth interrupted.

A guilty smile appeared on Gina's face. 'I know—but I did interfere again there. Monty is going to stay with Nic and Hannah. He knows them and has stayed there before. He'll be fine. So there is nothing to stop you going. Take it a day at a time, Ruth. See the clinic, see how you feel about the job and about Rico. You'll know if it is right. Honestly. And I hope it works out for you. You'd be family and I'll still get to see you often,' she finished, unshed tears shimmering in her eyes.

Ruth remained silent. She had much to think about and little time left to make a decision. Now, their heart-to-heart over, she helped Gina get changed into her going-away outfit and ushered her friend from the room. Seb was waiting impatiently, Rico by his side. Ruth's gaze clashed with his, and he moved to join her, his arm sliding protectively around her waist.

'All right?' he whispered.

Ruth nodded, hiding her continuing confusion. They met up with the rest of the guests and everyone went outside to see the happy couple on their way. Ruth knew Gina was looking forward to spending time at the villa on Elba where the fairy tale of her romance with Seb had begun—a romance which had mirrored that of her grandparents over half a century before. Seb had insisted that Maria go with them. Gina's grandmother had become good friends with Evelina, the local woman who acted as housekeeper for the Linardi family.

So lost was she in her thoughts that she was taken completely by surprise, automatically catching Gina's bouquet of fragrant sweet peas as it sailed through the air and landed in her arms. Her friend was laughing and gave her a cheeky wave. Ruth's gaze was drawn to Rico's and the heated expression in his eyes took her breath away.

Everything happened quickly after that. Rico's parents had to rush back to London for the evening function, but they were warm and friendly as they hugged her and told her again how welcome she would be in Florence. The rest of the guests also began to depart. Inside, Ruth helped Holly with Gina's things, which she was holding safely for her until she came home. As they took extra care packing away the stunning bridal dress, Holly hesitated.

'Ruth, honey, are you OK?' she asked, sky-blue eyes reflecting her concern.

'I'm fine.' Spontaneously and uncharacteristically, she gave her friend a hug. 'Gina explained what happened and why she didn't let anyone tell me.'

Holly smiled and hugged her back. 'Rico's as gorgeous as you said! I hope everything works out for you.'

'Thanks, Holly.'

Her friend's words were sincere, but Ruth

detected the sadness underlying them. She wished she could find a way to help Holly—who continued to break her heart over Gus—find the happiness she deserved, too.

Then it was over. Nic and Hannah gave Holly a lift home, and Ruth found herself alone with Rico. She felt ridiculously nervous as she walked by his side towards Seb's car, stowing the box containing Gina's wedding dress on the back seat. The short drive to her cottage seemed to take for ever, and she was tongue-tied, speaking only to give Rico directions. He, too, seemed preoccupied and disinclined to talk. Finally, he turned off the tree-lined rural lane and down the short, unpaved drive to her single-storey, whitewashed cottage with its slate roof and squat chimney.

'You live here?'

Rico's surprise drew her attention and made her defensive. 'Yes. What's wrong with it?'

'Nothing at all, *carissima*.' He caught her chin, his touch searing her skin as he tilted her face until their gazes met. Satisfaction gleamed in his hazel eyes. 'It is not what I had expected…but I am glad. Your home is beautiful.'

'Thank you. I like it.'

Rico's approval made her warm inside, although his reaction and his comments puzzled her. She led the way inside and left him to explore while she went to change. After hanging the obscenely expensive dress in its protective cover in her wardrobe, she pulled on dark grey trousers and a green cashmere jumper. Taking a deep breath, she went to find Rico who was studying the bookshelves that lined the twin recesses either side of the large open fireplace. He turned as she entered the room, and she noticed that he had taken off his tie and undone the top button of his shirt. Feeling awkward, Ruth hesitated, unsure what to say and do.

To cover her confusion, she went to the kitchen to make some tea. Aware that Rico had followed her, she busied herself with things to give her shaky hands something to do, covering her awkwardness by reverting to work and telling him about her meeting with Judith Warren the previous afternoon.

'She was so grateful for all the advice you gave and she feels there is light at the end of the tunnel now,' she finished, her breath catching as Rico closed the distance between them and took her hands in his.

'It is you who should take the credit—you listened to her, believed her, followed through for her.'

'Your help guided me in the right direction,' she insisted.

A smile curved Rico's sexy mouth and sent a jolt of desire right through her. 'What am I going to do with you?'

Ruth could think of a few wickedly pleasurably things she would like to experience with him again, but she held her tongue, still uncertain of the situation between them.

'We have things to discuss,' Rico continued, sobering, 'I meant all I said. I know you have the next two weeks off. Please, will you give me that time? Will you come to Florence to see the clinic and the work we do so you can decide if it is for you?'

The temptation was strong for so many reasons. But, again, Rico had given no indication that he wanted anything more than for her to work for him. She needed some clarification.

'This is just about the job?' she asked, hoping he would say no.

Something flashed in his eyes, but before she could decipher it, long dark lashes lowered to hide his expression. He released her, his hands moving behind his back to brace himself as he leaned on the worktop.

'Just the job, *sirena mia.*' His voice was without inflection as he said the words she had not wanted to hear. Then he added something in Italian that she did not understand. *'Per ora.'*

As the kettle boiled, Ruth turned away, lost in thought as she made the tea. Hope faded and disappointment bloomed inside her. He had said one night, and clearly he meant it. She was despondent, but then she thought of the advice Gina had given her…to take things slowly and not to give up. She had two weeks without other pressures to take time out and decide on the course of the rest of her life.

She had known from the moment she had first seen Rico that he was a threat to her. He had thrown her whole life and everything she believed about herself and what she wanted into turmoil. One thing was certain—she could never go back to how things had been before Rico.

Maybe she was making another mistake but she wanted to explore what might happen. She would go to Florence. She might be all kinds of a fool, but she would take the job—and whatever else came her way. Without Rico she would be miserable, whether she was in Scotland or Italy, so it was better to have a job that truly involved and challenged her. And who knew what else might happen?

Drawing in a steadying breath, Ruth turned to face him. 'I'll come to Florence.'

CHAPTER TEN

His hands thrust into the pockets of his trousers, Rico stood a short distance away, watching Ruth conduct a skin-prick test on six-year-old Simone Stevens. He experienced the customary rush of pride and desire just looking at her—feelings that grew stronger with each day that passed. Ostensibly, he was here in case Ruth required back-up during the procedure, but, as ever, she was in control and displaying her superb skills. Not just in clinical terms but in gaining the trust and co-operation of the little boy who had been anxious and tearful on arrival but who was now smiling and involved in what was going on.

Knowing Ruth thrived on the challenge of learning new things, he had thrown her in at the deep end when he had first brought her to the clinic over a week ago. He'd had every faith that she would cope. And she had—exceeding his highest expectations and justifying the confidence he had in her. Watching Ruth work was a special experience. She was comfortable in her professional role, warm and caring with patients, building rapport with them and making them feel that they mattered to her. Which they did. As he had realised when first meeting her, without her doctor persona to hide behind, much of her self-assurance drained away.

As if aware that he was observing her, Ruth glanced round. Their gazes met and held, and Rico felt the now-familiar electric connection zap through him. He smiled, giving a nod of approval in support of what she was doing, and his gut tightened when the mouth he had not kissed and tasted in far too long curved in an answering smile. Then she returned her attention to Simone, who was enduring the test designed to identify which allergens his body was reacting to with good humour.

'How is it that common things can cause harm to some people but not to others?' Simone's mother asked. Married to an American, Rosa Stevens's English was fluent but heavily accented—Simone had been raised speaking both languages.

Rico listened with interest and admiration as Ruth took time to help mother and son understand, her voice friendly and reassuring, but also authoritative.

'When the immune system thinks that the body is being attacked—when you have a cold or an infection, for example—it sends antibodies, called immunoglobulin E, or IgE, which travel through the bloodstream to find and counteract whatever is causing the damage. Like your Action Man soldier protecting you from dangerous invaders,' she added, and Simone, who was holding tightly on to his favourite toy with his free hand, nodded vigorously. 'Sometimes, though, the immune system makes a mistake and overreacts to a substance that is usually harmless and attacks the body's healthy tissue. Chemicals, including histamine, are released by blood cells, causing allergic reactions such as the rashes and other symptoms Simone's been having.'

There was no point in filling Rosa's head with information on the more extreme reactions experienced by some patients, for whom severe anaphylaxis could be fatal, and Rico was pleased that Ruth did not elaborate further at this stage.

'It is important for us to identify what substance or substances are responsible for Simone's problems,' Ruth continued. 'With so many potential triggers, it can take a while to discover the cause of the intolerance and allergic response, but once we know, we can work out a programme of desensitisation and treatment.'

Having applied a negative control and a histamine control, against which the results could later be assessed, Ruth began the main skin-prick test. One at a time, a small drop of each different allergen was administered to a separate square of the numbered grid that had been marked on Simone's arm. Next, Ruth used a lancet to prick the sample through the skin. A new sterile lancet was used for each individual site, preventing cross-contamination. The experienced nurse assisting her kept a careful written record and, in fifteen or twenty minutes, they would be able to examine Simone's arm and determine which, if any, allergens had caused a reaction.

A knock at the door diverted Rico's attention. Leaving Ruth to her task, he walked across the room and opened the door to discover his second in command waiting for him. Fifty years old and a father of five, Paolo Chiarini was short and rotund, with greying hair and kind brown eyes. A jovial man and top-class doctor, Paolo had been with him since the clinic had opened and Rico trusted him implicitly.

'*Ciao*, Rico,' the older man greeted him with an ever-present smile. 'Can I speak to you about

Valeria Di Maio? Her latest test results have come back.'

'Of course. Give me a moment.'

Rico returned to the group concentrating on Simone, and rested one hand on Ruth's shoulder. She tensed under his touch, but he forced himself to ignore the worry her reaction caused.

'I will be back shortly,' he told them. 'Call me if you need anything.'

After a moment's hesitation, Rico retreated. He had no qualms about leaving Ruth in charge. She didn't need him in a professional capacity. But he was becoming increasingly concerned that applied personally, too. Since the moment in her kitchen, when she had agreed to come to Florence, he had been on his best behaviour. Her stipulation that the trip was just about the job had upset him, but he had hidden his disappointment—and he had had his hands behind his back and his fingers crossed as he had lied before adding *'Per ora'*…meaning 'for now'. Not that his plan to win Ruth round was making any headway.

It was killing him not being able to touch her, to hold her, to kiss her, to make love to her. But she had needed time and he had been determined he would give it to her. It was proving much harder than he had imagined. Things had happened so fast when they had met and he had allowed his heart to rule his head. In consequence he had made the mistake of rushing her. He had still not discovered why Ruth had run. One possibility was that the intensity of what they had shared had scared her. He understood that, especially given her past. The other possibility—that she didn't feel the same way he did—nagged at him. Had he really misjudged things that badly? That Ruth didn't feel the same connection had been given more credence by her skittishness these last ten days and the distance she kept between them.

'Ruth is extraordinary,' Paolo ventured in Italian, curtailing Rico's introspection.

'Yes, she is.'

As he stepped out of the room, Rico allowed himself one last lingering look at the woman who had turned his world upside down, then he closed the door. As well as proving her worth as a doctor, and her potential for excelling in the fields of immunology and allergy, Ruth had won the hearts of all the clinic staff.

'Is she going to stay?'

Rico shrugged his shoulders, trying to hide how important Ruth's decision was to him— and not because of the job. 'I don't know. All we can do is hope.'

'You must talk to her. She will do wonders here when trained.' The older man paused a moment, a speculative expression in his brown eyes. 'It is obvious that you care for her. Speaking as your friend, do not let Ruth slip through your fingers.'

'I am doing my best, Paolo.'

But was his best good enough? Ruth was worth any effort or sacrifice and, no matter the cost to himself, he was trying to do the right thing and not push her too far again. But he was troubled. The only physical contact he had managed was holding hands on the sightseeing trips they had shared. Increasingly Ruth was avoiding every casual touch and it was playing havoc with his hope and confidence that he could eventually win her round.

He didn't know what he would do if Ruth decided that a career change was not for her. Or how he could bear it if she accepted the job but rejected him. One thing was certain. He was running out of time. It was Wednesday. And Ruth was due to meet up with Seb, Gina and Maria when they came over from Elba on Sunday morning. Then they would fly back to Scotland together.

What the hell was he going to do?

* * *

'You are enjoying the work at the clinic, *mia cara*?' Sofia queried.

'Very much,' Ruth answered truthfully. 'I am learning so much every day. And everyone has been kind. I just wish that I spoke the language so that I could help more.'

Sofia smiled and patted her hand. 'You will be surprised how quickly you pick it up when you are living here full time. Besides Italian, all the clinic staff speak English and at least one other language—patients of many nationalities come to the clinic for help. Language will not be a barrier for you.'

Unsure what to say, Ruth remained silent. Nothing had yet been decided about her future but Sofia's words, taking it for granted that she would stay, brought a mix of nervousness, confusion and excitement. They were sitting out on the veranda at the rear of the Linardi family's luxurious Florentine villa, having enjoyed a light meal at the end of another busy day.

Ruth was tired but professionally satisfied. All had gone well with little Simone's tests, and they were closer to finding an answer and identifying what was causing his symptoms. Later, she had also learned that there was news on Valeria Di Maio's test results. Valeria was the woman Rico had told her about at the conference, the new patient with severe photosensitivity. Hers had been the first case Rico had taken on when they had arrived in Florence after the wedding, and Ruth had found herself in the thick of things straight away.

Having done some research after Rico had first mentioned the woman's symptoms, Ruth had ventured an opinion during a clinic meeting on Valeria's case, that the problem could be systemic lupus erythematosus, or SLE. The room had fallen silent and she had been uncomfortably aware that everyone was staring at her. It had probably only been a few seconds before Paolo and the other staff had praised her, but to Ruth it had felt like an hour, and her heart had threatened to jump right out of her chest. Then she had looked at Rico. She would never forget the warmth of his smile or the approval in his hazel eyes.

'Well done, Ruth.' Although understated, Rico's words and the tone of his voice had made her glow. 'SLE is a great mimic,' he had continued. 'Many patients do not fit the criteria of the disease and many doctors are confused and misled by the variety and often complex combination of symptoms. No two cases are the same.

Because of this, eleven classic criteria were established to help aid the diagnosis. There are exceptions, of course, but if a patient has four or more of these, then it suggests systemic lupus is likely.'

Today, the final results from the battery of tests Valeria had undergone had come back, confirming photosensitivity, blood-count abnormalities, mucous-membrane ulcers, a positive antinuclear antibody or ANA test, and discoid skin rash. In other words, Valeria satisfied five of the eleven classic criteria, a strong guide that the diagnosis of SLE was correct. There was no cure, and she had a difficult journey ahead of her, but Ruth knew the woman was in the very best place to receive first-class care, support and treatment to relieve her symptoms. The plan would be to prevent increases in the level of autoimmune activity and to decrease inflammation, so protecting the body's organs and minimising periods when the disease was active.

The clinic itself was fabulous, the best she had ever seen. The facilities were outstanding. And so were the staff. All of them had welcomed her openly and had gone out of their way to help her find her feet and settle in, expressing their hope that she would decide to join them on a permanent basis. It was what Ruth wanted, too. Rico's enthusiasm was infectious. She had learned so much in the last ten days, and her respect for him as a doctor was boundless. The chance to change direction and work with Rico was a once-in-a-lifetime opportunity. And Rico was a once-in-a-lifetime man.

The job was hers for the taking.

The man, she feared, was not.

She was confused. At work, Rico was patient, informative, supportive and encouraging. He challenged her, but she thrived on it, absorbing as much knowledge from him as she could. Away from work, he was attentive, funny and considerate. He had determined that her trip was not all about work, and ensured they take time each day for sightseeing so he could show her the city. As well as customary tourist venues—from the impressive cathedral and the treasures in the famous Uffizi gallery to the magnificent statue of Michelangelo's David, which stood in the square outside the town hall as defender of the city, and the plethora of shops on the Ponte Vecchio, many of them selling gold and jewellery—Rico had shown her many exquisite things off the beaten track that she would never have found alone. They had walked for hours, recharging their batteries with ice cream or coffee and cake. He had held her hand, taken care of her, devoted time to her, and treated her like a sister or best friend. He hadn't kissed her…or given any sign that he wanted to. While her awareness of him magnified and her body yearned for his, he appeared to have forgotten that their explosive night of passion had ever happened.

Rico had not only taken her in at the clinic, he had insisted that she live in his home. He had been the perfect host and the perfect gentleman. And she had slept alone every night. Or had tried to sleep. It had proved nearly impossible when she ached so much with wanting him. His room was mere feet away from hers, but they might have been on different continents for the distance there was between them. Being so close to him and yet so far away was as difficult as she had expected it would be. She wanted to go to him, to ask for more, but she didn't have the confidence to do it. And so she had devoted herself to the clinic and to learning.

'Could you live here, *mia cara*? What do you think of our city?'

Easily, was the quick answer to the first question from Sofia that drew Ruth from her thoughts. Rico and his father were yet to join them and she was alone with Rico's mother and his grandmother, Emanuela. The elderly lady was a real character, and it was touching to see the bond Rico shared with her. An ear infection, now much improved, had prevented her flying to Scotland for Seb and Gina's wedding, but she had been keen to hear all about it. And she had eagerly shown Ruth photographs of the family villa where Seb, Gina and Maria were staying.

'I *love* Florence,' Ruth answered with enthusiasm. 'It's a beautiful city. The art and architecture are amazing, and the history is fascinating. I've thoroughly enjoyed walking by the river, doing some window-shopping, and exploring the museums, galleries and chapels. I don't think I could see all I wanted to in a lifetime.'

Living here wasn't the problem. She would do it in a heartbeat. She *did* love Florence, just as she loved the job, loved Rico's family—who had shown her the acceptance and affection she had never known from her own parents—and she loved Rico. Everything had happened so fast and been so intense between them from the start, and one benefit of the last ten days had been time. Time, without other pressures or expectations, to slow things down, which had allowed her to get to know Rico as a person—as well as a superb doctor. And having done so, she could no longer deny her real feelings. Not to herself. But how could she reconcile things? How could she stay and take the job that excited her so much when it meant seeing Rico all the time and knowing she could never have him? Yet the thought of giving it all up was heart-breaking.

'I think if I lived here all the time, I would end up the size of a house,' she continued, trying to make light of things.

Emanuela waved a hand to dismiss her suggestion. 'You will never be anything but beautiful to us.'

'I've become addicted to the *gelato*,' Ruth explained, trying to blink away the tears that the elderly woman's words had caused. 'There are so many flavours to try. Then I discovered *zuccotto*!' She moaned theatrically, making Sofia chuckle and Emanuela laugh aloud and clap her hands in delight. 'And there are Luciana's spectacular chestnut pancakes.'

Rico's housekeeper, Luciana Malavolti, who cared for the inside of the house with as much dedication as her husband, Alessandro, cared for the outside, had promised to show her how to make the pancakes. Chestnuts were a local crop, and some were made into a flour that was used for baking and in all sorts of recipes.

'Tuscan gastronomy may be more simple than that of some other regions, but to the people here, food is an art,' Emanuela told her.

The food might be considered simple, but it was delicious…and plentiful! Ruth was getting used to the different way things were done in Italy. Breakfast, as she knew it, was almost non-existent, little more than a coffee on the run, while dinner at night was light and often eaten very late. At lunchtime, however, everything seemed to shut down and people came together to relax and enjoy a big meal with many courses.

Ruth was savouring new food experiences but, as she had told Sofia and Emanuela, the things she was finding it impossible to resist were the outstanding home-made *gelato*, or ice cream and the *zuccotto*…a dome-shaped sponge cake filled with a mixture of almonds, hazelnuts, chocolate and cream. The first time she had tasted it she thought she had died and gone to heaven!

The sound of the villa's entryphone pierced the silence on the terrace, and Sofia excused herself, rising gracefully from her chair and heading indoors. Ruth looked out into the rapidly darkening night, enjoying the lights of the city. She very much hoped this was not the last time she would be able to visit the Linardis in their lovely home.

'We have a moment alone. May I speak with you, Ruth?'

'Of course,' she responded, taken by surprise at the serious tone of Emanuela's voice.

'I may be an old woman, but my eyes still function!' A customary chuckle rumbled from inside her. 'I see how you look at Riccardo.'

Ruth blushed and her heart sank. Clearly she had not been as adept at hiding her feelings as she had thought. 'I—'

Emanuela took her hand. 'Do not look so worried, *figliola*. It would make me very happy to see you together.'

'Rico doesn't feel that way about me.' Somehow she forced the words out, even though saying them tore at her heart. 'I'm just here for the job.'

'*Sciocchezze*! What nonsense! If Riccardo only wanted for you to work at the clinic, why would he have you live at his house out of the city?' the elderly lady protested with spirit.

'But—'

'Riccardo has never taken another woman to his home. Does that not tell you something?'

Ruth shook her head, puzzled because Emanuela's comments were at odds with Rico's behaviour. 'I don't know.'

'You fear rejection, yes?' the woman asked, giving her fingers a gentle squeeze.

Overcome by her insight and the affection she had shown her, Ruth nodded.

'Take my advice, *figliola*. Do not risk losing what is within your grasp. Some things are not as they seem,' she added mysteriously. 'Have the courage to reach for what you want. I think you will be surprised by the results!'

'Ruth is doing well at the clinic?'

'Very well.' His answer to his father's question was a gross understatement, Rico allowed. He stood at the window in the study, watching Ruth talk with Nonna Emanuela as they sat on the terrace. 'I have never met anyone as gifted as Ruth. She is a remarkably quick learner and wonderful with patients.'

'Do you not think it is time to stop tiptoeing around?' his father asked.

Frowning, Rico dragged the fingers of one hand through his hair and finally turned away from the view outside the window. 'What do you mean, Papà?'

'When you first introduced us in Scotland, you said that Ruth was the woman you hoped to marry.'

'That is so.' He sighed and sank down on to a chair on the other side of the desk. 'But Ruth is only interested in the job.'

His father's sudden bark of laughter took him by surprise. 'Rico!'

'What?' he demanded, frustration making him uncharacteristically irritable.

'For the first time you are truly in love. You have found the woman of your heart.' The words hit home, and he listened as his father continued. 'Do not allow it to blind you and stop you from seeing what is right before your eyes.'

Rico's confused frown deepened. 'How do you mean… blind me?'

Before his father could reply, the door opened and his mother stepped in, calling him to see the visitor who needed some advice. As they left the study together, his father draped an arm around his shoulders.

'Go home, *figlio mio*,' he advised with a smile. 'Claim your woman!'

Rico watched his parents walk away, then he went to the terrace to fetch Ruth.

'You are ready to go?' he asked, agitation making his voice brusquer than normal.

'Yes, all right.'

As Ruth gathered her things, he kissed Nonna Emanuela, who scowled at him and looked as if she wanted to scold him, just as she had done when he had been a boy. Ruth seemed even more on edge and skittish than before as they took their leave and headed out to the car. He remembered her reaction when they had picked his black Ferrari up at the airport, and how she had teased him about it.

'I thought you weren't interested in luxuries and ostentatious extravagance!'

'My car is my one indulgence, my only weakness,' he had told her.

As he drove out of the city and headed towards his home, he knew that was no longer true. Ruth had become his weakness. It had been a constant battle not to give in to the temptation to whisk her off and seduce her, to make her stay with *him* and damn the job. He thought of the advice he had been given that day. Both Paolo and his father had urged him to act. What did they see that he was missing? And why did they talk in riddles instead of telling him something useful?

The tension increased with each kilometre they travelled out of Florence and into the countryside. Ruth felt jumpy and troubled. Searching for a safe subject, she thought of something and made an effort to break the awkward silence.

'I didn't get the chance to tell you earlier, Rico, but I had an email this afternoon from Mr and Mrs Michaels.' She had been so pleased to hear from the parents of the young man who had suffered such nasty burns during the accident at the restaurant overlooking Morecambe Bay. 'Jamie is settled at the specialist burns unit. The doctors are pleased with his progress and confident about his recovery.'

'That is very good news. I hope he continues to do well.'

Rather than easing the charged atmosphere, her topic of conversation seemed only to have added to it. It had certainly reminded her of the restaurant. And the conference. And their passionate night. Ruth felt Rico's gaze flick to her, glad he could not see her clearly in the dimness inside the car, and she turned her head to stare unseeingly through the side window, her hands knotted together in her lap.

The rest of the journey was completed in silence, but Ruth felt the electricity arcing between them. It did nothing to calm her nerves. She anticipated arriving at Rico's house and thought back to the first time she had come here—the Sunday after the wedding, following their flight from Scotland to Florence.

Rico's comments when he had seen where she lived in Strathlochan had made sense as soon as they had reached his home. Located in the Mugello, the beautiful area to the north-east of Florence in the watershed of the Apennines, the old single-storey house, built in local honey-coloured stone—which, she had discovered, Rico had restored himself—was set amongst wooded hills and rolling fields.

The oldest part of the house dated back to the fourteenth century, and had been sympathetically extended over the years, keeping its original beams and terracotta floors. Secluded and private, it was an Italian version of her own home. It was bigger, of course, with more expansive views, and it had a swimming pool, but the similarities were striking.

Rico's land extended over a hundred acres, and linked up with one of the many trekking trails. Ruth had enjoyed a long walk with Rico the previous weekend and had seen wild boar and roe deer, as well as many other examples of the area's extensive fauna and flora. What she longed to see were the wolves that Rico had told her lived in the Casentino Forests National Park, a protected area in the Apennines that spanned the borders of Tuscany and Emilia-Romagna.

As with the city of Florence itself, it would take her a lifetime to explore this landscape, from the high ridges, waterfalls and verdant valleys to the wildflower meadows and woods of oak, beech and chestnut. Did she have a lifetime here?

Everything about Rico's home, and the region in which it was set, had taken her breath away. She had immediately felt comfortable and at peace. As if she belonged here. It had been a struggle these last few days to remember that even if she took the job at Rico's clinic, this wonderful place was *not* her home. Just as Rico was not her man. But, oh, how she wished she had the right to lay claim to both.

Emanuela had told her that Rico had never brought another woman here. Was that true? And, if so, had he just asked her to stay because he wanted to persuade her to work for him? When she had met Rico's housekeeper for the first time, Luciana had been surprised that he had brought a guest to stay, Ruth recalled, but she had not thought anything of it at the time. And whatever Rico had told Luciana in Italian had pleased the older woman, who had been warm and friendly. As had her husband Alessandro. The couple lived in a small cottage out of sight of the main house. Both of them were devoted to Rico, who had provided them with work and a place to stay when they had fallen on hard times.

Now, as the headlights picked out the gate-posts that marked the entrance to the drive, Rico turned the sleek Ferrari between them and moved towards the house, hidden from view beyond the trees. Ruth sucked in a shaky breath, uncertain of his mood. He seemed distracted, unsettled, which only increased her own unease and confusion. Was he regretting having her here? If she stayed on at the clinic, she would have to find her own place. What would it feel like to live alone in Florence and only see Rico at work? The thought depressed her.

Her chest felt tight, and she was acutely conscious of him as he walked beside her to the front door and unlocked it, reaching inside to switch on the light. The action brought him close enough for her to catch a tantalising hint of his cedar scent and the warm maleness of him.

Disturbed by her increasing awareness of him and need for him, Ruth stepped hastily away, putting some distance between them.

'Ruth…'

'I'm really tired,' she lied, unable to meet his gaze as she moved towards the bedroom wing. 'I'm going to get an early night.'

She escaped before he could detain her, and, on reaching her room, she closed the door and leaned back against it. Have courage, Emanuela had told her. And what had she done? Scuttled away like a frightened mouse. Cursing herself, she went to have a quick shower.

After putting on a thin nightdress, all she needed in the warmer temperatures in Italy, Ruth sat on the bed, knowing she was never going to be able to sleep. Rico was all she could think about. Gina's words, encouraging her to fight for him if he was what she wanted, returned to her. And she *did* want him. Which meant she would have to try and do something she had never done before. Seduce a man.

Taking her friend's and Emanuela's advice would not be easy, especially with her lack of experience. It was true that she feared Rico's rejection. And it would mean taking a huge risk. But she had nothing more to lose. She needed to know if there was any chance of something more than a job and a one-night memory between them.

Restless, and needing to clear her head, Ruth

opened the French window and stepped out onto the deserted terrace that overlooked the swimming pool and, in daylight, the magnificent vista. Everything was quiet and still, and the warm breeze felt good against her skin. Gazing out into the night, with only the pool's edging lights and the glow from her room breaking the darkness, she tried to decide what to do. If she succeeded in working out a plan of action, would she have the courage to see it through?

CHAPTER ELEVEN

'DIO!'

Restless and frustrated, his mind troubled, Rico turned over and thumped his pillow. Ruth had been distracted and even more jumpy that evening, and she had not been able to retreat to her room fast enough when they had arrived home, confounding his attempts to speak to her. He was no closer to a solution about what to do and the increasing tension was almost more than he could bear.

Linking his hands behind his head, he lay on his back and stared up at the ceiling. He had tried his best to be patient, knowing that Ruth needed time and understanding, but things were not working out as he had hoped and his restraint was wearing thin. Although he still had not grasped exactly what his father had been trying to tell him, his basic message had echoed that of Paolo's earlier in the day. Time was running out. If he wanted Ruth—and he did—

then he was going to have to act and damn the consequences.

He huffed out a breath. Never had he felt so uncertain, and scared, in his life before. He had been so sure that Ruth felt the same connection he did, and that their extraordinary night together had sealed the bond between them. But finding her gone the next morning had stripped away his confidence and left him with doubts— doubts that Ruth's skittish behaviour these last ten days had done nothing to allay.

Midnight came and he was still tossing and turning. He and Ruth had been circling around each other for far too long. He needed to know one way or another where things stood between them. And if that meant laying all his cards on the table and facing ultimate rejection, it was a risk he was going to have to take.

Rising from the bed, he pulled on swim shorts, opened the door that led from his bedroom to the terrace, and stepped outside. It was a balmy night, the temperature unusually warm for May. Honeysuckle and jasmine climbed the wooden frame and provided a living canopy over the terrace, their scent perfuming the air. Cloud layered the sky, blocking out most of the stars.

Hoping a swim would clear his head, cool his

libido, and help him formulate a new plan, he took a step towards the pool, but a sound alerted him and he looked round, stopping dead in his tracks when he discovered he was not alone. Ruth was leaning against the railing further along the terrace.

As she stepped back, a shaft of light spilling from the open door behind her rendered her flimsy night slip transparent, revealing her naked outline beneath and rocketing his temperature up even higher. Her hair encased her face in a halo of pale gold. His body reacted in an inevitable way. As if in slow motion, Ruth looked up and saw him. And there, in that unguarded moment, her expression unmasked and her emotions laid bare, he saw what he had been waiting and hoping for—desire, longing and the same desperate yearning that overwhelmed him.

'Ruth…'

The last threads of his control snapped.

'*Maledizione*! To hell with patience.'

With purposeful strides, he began to close the gap between them. Paolo and his father had been right. It was time to claim his woman.

Engrossed in her thoughts, Ruth ceased her pacing and rested her hands on the wooden railing, watching the shifting shadows and flickers of light across the gently undulating surface of the pool several feet away. A noise impinged on her consciousness and she looked up, searching for the source of the sound. She stepped back, her gaze sweeping from the open door to her room nearby, along the wall of the house to Rico's room, which had been in darkness a short while before. Now the door was open and the light from within held Rico in its glow.

Ruth stifled a gasp of surprise, one hand rising to her throat where she could feel the rapidly accelerating beat of her heart. He was superb. She could not drag her gaze from the picture he presented, clad only in black swim briefs—like an ancient god, a figure of masculinity far more perfect even than Michelangelo's David. Ruth's mouth went dry, her lungs constricted, and her heart pounded against her ribs. Longing and desire consumed her, too much to contain after days of trying to hide how she felt about him.

'Ruth...'

Her name whispered softly to her on the breeze. Then she heard Rico's curse in the stillness of the night, and everything in her tightened and trembled as he strode towards her. The impatience and naked hunger in his eyes stole her breath. He looked like a man who refused to be denied. Excitement throbbed deep inside her. Her stomach clenched and the ache of need intensified beyond bearing. Without even realising she was moving, she stepped to meet him.

There was no time to think. No time to question the future. All that mattered was the here and now, and the raging, desperate, painful need that only he could assuage. She wanted him. *So* badly.

Bodies collided. Mouths met...open, hot, hungry. Passion exploded. Rico fisted one hand in her hair, angling her head for the deepest fit. His other hand held her rear, and pulled her tight against him. She wriggled, needing to be closer still, swallowing his moan as she rubbed against the hard evidence of his arousal.

The kiss was uncompromising, demanding, unrestrained, igniting the flames that had been smouldering just beneath the surface. Ruth clung to him, her fingers savouring warm male flesh as they roamed across his shoulders, down his back, and everywhere she could reach, eager to relearn his body, urgently needing to touch all of him. His masculine scent mingled with exotic cedar—a combination that was uniquely Rico, familiar and arousing. Her tongue danced and duelled with his. His taste intoxicated her. How had she survived the last two weeks without this?

Unable to bear anything at all between them, her questing fingers freed him from the restriction of the briefs, and she struggled to push the clinging fabric down as far as she could without breaking the kiss. Rico helped her, impatiently working them off and kicking them away, groaning when her fingers reclaimed him, and she boldly stroked and shaped and teased him.

His hands were equally busy, skimming over her, setting every particle of her on fire. But it wasn't enough. She needed to feel them against her skin. He clearly had the same thought, and Ruth gasped as the sound of ripping fabric rent the air. She felt the whisper of fresh air on her heated flesh as Rico dispensed with the tattered remains of her nightdress. Then his hands were on her, his knowing, urgent caresses driving her higher.

Excitement building, she clasped his shoulders as he walked her back and lifted her until she was sitting on the wide wooden railing. He stepped between her parted thighs and she ran her hands down his back to his taut rear, her fingers tightening as she urged him closer, desperate for him to ease the terrible hollow ache that was clamouring deep within her.

He broke the wild kiss, his mouth working down her throat, lips sucking, teeth nipping, his tongue salving the erotic sting.

'Please, Rico,' she begged, her breathing ragged, her pulse racing. *'Please.'*

His stubbled jaw grazed across her skin…a delicious caress that drove her wild. She writhed against him, crying out as his mouth moved to one of her breasts and drew the swollen, sensitised peak inside, sucking strongly. The dart of pleasure was so intense that her fingers speared into the luxuriant strands of his hair, trying to pull him closer and push him away at the same time.

Sobbing, Ruth wrapped her legs around his hips, drawing him more tightly to her. She needed him—now. As his mouth released her nipple, and he kissed his way across to lavish the same torturous attention on its twin, clever, wicked fingers zeroed in to the very heart of her, finding her more than ready for him.

'I need you, *sirena mia.*' His voice was low, rough, sexy.

Ruth's urgency matched his and she pleaded

with him to hurry. 'Yes! Rico… Here. Now, please.'

Her words trailed off as he complied with her demands, and Ruth held on to him as he united them, crying out at the wonder of experiencing this again. It was wild, frantic, desperate. Ruth lost herself in the magic of the moment, craving more, giving him everything as they moved together, the sense of fullness, the erotic friction, the searing pleasure building and building as their rhythm increased, rushing them both towards the inevitable conclusion.

Ruth didn't want this most shattering, incredible experience ever to end. She tightened her legs and wrapped her arms around him, her hands clinging as she tried to find purchase on his slick hot skin.

'Don't stop, don't stop, don't stop…' Sobbing, she arched into him, overcome by the intensity of what they were sharing.

Rico's arm around her hips bound her to him, and his free hand returned to her hair, his fingers tangling in the loose strands as he buried his face in her neck, his whispered words muffled against her skin.

'Come with me, *sirena mia.*'

However much she wanted to prolong the bliss

of making love with him, she couldn't stop her body responding to the demands of his. The pleasure built, wave after impossible wave, until it finally crested, crashing over her with such force it threatened to sweep her away. Rico was her anchor and she was his. They clung to each other as they plunged over the edge of the precipice, lost in the whirling vortex, spinning out of control as the ecstasy consumed them.

Ruth had no idea how much time passed before some kind of thought process was possible again. She couldn't move, and she certainly couldn't speak. Her head dropped to his shoulder and with every ragged breath she inhaled his scent. Every part of her was shaking and trembling. Her heart was pounding. So was Rico's. She could feel it where his chest pressed against hers. He still held her close, and she was grateful, because the more reality began to intrude the more scared she became about what happened next.

What, if anything, had this meant to Rico? She closed her eyes and snuggled against him, trying to push her worries from her mind. His mouth closed on her shoulder, lips brushing, teeth nibbling, tongue lazily stroking. Ruth quivered, resting against him, her legs relaxing but not unwinding. Far too soon, though, Rico drew back and she reluctantly released him. His hands cupped her face, a serious expression in his hazel eyes as he looked at her.

'Are you all right?'

Ruth nodded, not at all sure that she was. It depended on what Rico said next—whether this was another one-off night, or something more. At this point she was so confused...and so in love with him that she would take any scraps that fell from the table.

'I am sorry, *sirena mia*,' he murmured, his voice rough.

Ruth tensed at the apology, upset that he regretted what they had just done. She shook her head, unable to speak, unable to meet his gaze in case she saw rejection in his eyes.

'We didn't use anything,' Rico continued, his explanation easing some of her initial anxiety. 'I have *never* forgotten protection before...but I've never had this urgent need before, either.'

'I'm on the Pill for health reasons.'

Rather than reassuring, her words appeared to disturb him, his brow knotting in a frown. 'You are not well? Something is wrong?'

'I'm fine.' She smiled, warmed by his obvious

concern. 'My cycle has never been regular, that's all.'

Given both their histories—neither of them having been with anyone else for a long time, and never unprotected before—and having had regular health checks, they knew they were clear of any transmittable infection. And, while not impossible, an unplanned pregnancy was highly unlikely. The sudden rush of disappointment shocked her. She had never considered children, had never imagined, after Adam, that she would be with another man. Now, though, she realised how much she wanted Rico's baby.

As he helped her down from the railing, she wobbled alarmingly, reaction setting in and her legs refusing to obey her. He swung her up into his arms, but Ruth didn't protest…it was where she wanted to be, after all. And where she hoped to stay for as long as possible.

Rico carried a drowsy Ruth to his room and gently tucked her into his bed before sliding in beside her and cradling her in his arms. Nuzzling his face against her, he breathed in the fragrance of lavender and warm, aroused, sated woman. He was not surprised that she felt so shaky. Or so tired. He felt the same. That he had been so lost he had forgotten protection for the first time ever was a shock. More so was the urgent desire to see Ruth bloom and grow with their child.

As she napped, Rico remained wide awake, reliving over again the experience they had just shared. He could not put into words how incredible it had been. But until he was able to have a serious talk with Ruth about the future, the fear would linger that she did not feel the same way he did. She had been a willing participant in their wild and frantic love-making, but he had not imagined her withdrawal afterwards, or the way she had refused to meet his gaze. He loved her with everything in him, and the fact that he still didn't know what she wanted, even whether she would accept the job and stay in Florence, made him sick with nerves and doubt.

Propping himself on one elbow, he lay on his side and studied Ruth's face in the glow from the bedside lamp. She was so beautiful, it took his breath away just to look at her. Her skin was flawless, her bone structure perfect. Unable to resist the temptation, he used one fingertip to lightly trace the haphazard trail of freckles that dusted her cheekbones and the bridge of her nose. Long dusky lashes flickered and he felt his pulse throb in his veins as they slowly parted to reveal slumberous green eyes.

'Hi,' he whispered, his voice rough.

'Hi. I…' Her words trailed off, a faint tinge of colour washing her cheeks as his questing finger moved to outline the shape of her mouth. 'Rico…'

Ruth turned her head just enough so that his finger slid between her parted lips, and his breath caught as she sucked on it, lightly grazing with her teeth. The desire that had undone him earlier returned to her eyes, unguarded as she watched him with the kind of yearning that caused his body to respond in the most elemental way. He tried to remember that he needed to talk to her, but she released his finger, a new boldness evident as she sank the fingers of one hand into his hair and drew him down, her lips nibbling on his.

He needed no second invitation. Pulling her into his arms, he rolled over so that she was on top of him, giving himself up to the magic that always flared between them, savouring her taste, her scent, the feel of her silky soft skin gliding against his in a full body caress. He wanted her, needed her. And he was about to show her just how much when she caught his wrists, halting him.

'Ruth?'

He looked up, momentarily concerned, but then words failed him and every nerve-ending went on red alert at the wicked expression in her eyes and sexy smile that curved lips still full from their wildly erotic kisses.

'My turn.'

Rico thought his heart would beat right out of his chest as she lowered her head and traced the tip of her tongue from the hollow of his throat down his chest. *Mio Dio!* He fought for control, giving himself up to the magic of her delicious seduction, more than aware how significant this moment was given her past belief that she was a failure as a woman, unable to give or receive pleasure. That she now had the confidence to explore her desires and her sensual nature, to ask for and take what she wanted, was a huge break-through and one that left his chest tight with emotion. Before she took him past the point of no return, she paused a moment, looking up to meet his gaze, and he saw the knowledge in her eyes, the recognition of the significance of what they were sharing. And then he couldn't think any more as Ruth's hands and mouth took him to paradise.

An endless time later, when he had gained a second wind, he devoted himself to Ruth and to showing her once more that she could receive as much pleasure as she gave. He lingered over every reactive particle of her skin, savouring her taste, revelling in the sounds she couldn't contain. And while he couldn't bear to believe that this might be the last chance he had to make love to her, he was going to show her in every way possible how much she was loved and cherished. Discussions about the future would have to wait a while longer.

'Rico?'

'I am here, *sirena mia.*'

Ruth had lost all track of time, but as her eyes opened she saw that it was still dark outside. She was cradled in Rico's arms and one of his hands was stroking her hair. Every cell in her body hummed with sensation. He had made love to her again, endlessly, and with such exquisite tenderness it had brought tears to her eyes. Now she looked at him, finding him propped up on the pillows.

'Can't you sleep?' she asked, resting against him, soothed and aroused as his fingers slid under her tousled fall of hair and massaged mini circles on her skin.

'I am afraid to go to sleep.'

'Afraid?' His admission startled her. She frowned, puzzled and concerned. 'Why?'

'In case I wake up and find you gone again.'

Tears stung her eyes. 'Rico—'

'Why, Ruth? What happened to make you run?' The tone of his voice revealed his hurt and confusion, and Ruth's guilt intensified. 'I thought you had been as involved as me in what we had. What did I do wrong?'

'Nothing!' she exclaimed in shock.

'Ruth…'

She shook her head, taking his free hand in both of hers. 'It wasn't that. It wasn't you, Rico.'

'Then *why* did you go?'

Ruth bit her lip in indecision. She had come this far, and now was the time, however difficult she found it, to follow Gina's and Emanula's advice and fight for the man she loved. To do that, she had to lay her heart—and her insecurities—on the line. 'You said we had one night only and—'

'What are you talking about?' Rico interrupted, looking genuinely aghast.

'I didn't know what to do,' she confided, her voice wavering. 'Being with you was beyond anything I had ever experienced.' She felt a blush warm her cheeks and lowered her lashes, unable to look into Rico's eyes. 'I'd thought I could handle it, but when I woke up, I knew I couldn't. I didn't know how to say goodbye, or how to go on seeing you, talking to you about the job, and knowing I could never be with you again.'

'Madre di Dio!' He freed his hand from hers and tilted her chin, bringing her gaze back to his. 'No, *sirena mia*. I never said one night only,' he protested, and she could not doubt the sincerity in his voice or his eyes. 'How could you think that?'

Ruth swallowed, wondering if she had, indeed, made a terrible mistake. 'You asked me to give you one night. I thought that was what you meant. It's not like I'd had a lot of experience at that kind of thing,' she added, surprised when her spirited defence drew a dimpled smile from Rico, one that caused her heart to skip and tightened the ever-present ache of need inside her, a need that even the last hours of love-making had not begun to satisfy.

'I wanted you to give me that night so I could show you how special you were, and that what we had together was unique and incredible. Not one night *only*.'

'Oh!' Ruth pressed a hand to her throat, stunned at what he had said and how she had completely misunderstood. 'But I asked you if you wanted me to come to Florence just for the job, and you said yes.'

Rico groaned, slapping his palm to his forehead in a gesture of exasperation. 'No, *sirena mia*! That is not so.'

'But—' He pressed two fingers to her lips to silence her.

'You had run once. I did not know why. You asked me for some time. Then we unexpectedly met again at the wedding, a coincidence neither of us had imagined or prepared for.' Ruth nodded—that was certainly true. 'When you asked if coming to Florence was just about the job, I thought that was what *you* wanted. I nearly said no, because that was not what I had hoped for, but I was scared you would not come at all. So I lied and said yes,' he confided with another endearing smile, telling her what his Italian words had meant. 'I knew I had made the mistake of rushing you the first time we were together, so I thought that once you were here in Florence, I could get close to you again and go slowly so as not to scare you. But every time I touched you, you flinched away, and I was beginning to despair, to think that I had got everything wrong and that you were not attracted to me, that our night together had been a disappointment for you.'

Ruth was speechless. She tried to absorb all he had told her, hope and joy blooming inside her. Maybe this was not a short-term fling after all. As for his concern that making love with him had been a disappointment! Ruth did not know how to adequately put into words what being with him was like and how he had changed her life and her belief in herself.

As he held her, she thought back over what he had said. 'I was confused, Rico. We came to Florence and you were acting like a friend or a brother, as if nothing had ever happened between us. I pulled away because I was worried I would give in to temptation and rip your clothes off,' she teased with a new-found confidence in herself as a woman.

'*Sirena mia*, I will always be your friend. But a brother? That is not what I had in mind,' he murmured, the sexy roughness of his voice and wicked look in his eyes fanning the flames of desire inside her. 'And you can rip my clothes off any time you like.'

Being with Rico made her light-hearted and light-headed, and brought out her own playful side. 'You aren't wearing any.'

'Neither are you,' he observed, his hands skimming her body, making her tingle.

She quirked an eyebrow at him. 'What are we going to do about it?'

'I have an idea.' Catching her by surprise, he rolled off the bed and scooped her up in his arms.

Laughing, she clung on to his shoulders. 'Where are we going?'

'You have to be punished for tormenting me so, *carissima*,' he threatened with mock annoyance. 'There is one place suitable for you.'

Excitement coursed through her as he headed out on to the terrace where they had found each other again a few short hours ago. There was a gleam in his eyes, and she pretended to be worried. 'I'm trembling.'

'You will soon be more than trembling, *sirena mia*.' The sexy rumble of his voice made her do just that. He paused and adjusted her in his arms. 'Hold on.'

Realising what he was going to do she slid her arms around his neck. 'Rico!' She squealed as he jumped into the pool.

Rico was happy to let Ruth play in the water for a while. It was such a joy to see this side of her, to hear her unrestrained laughter and to look into her stunning green eyes and find them free of shadows.

The discoveries he had made in the last half an

hour were taking a while to sink in. How could they have misunderstood each other so completely? He did not know. But it had taught him a valuable lesson. From now on he would make sure that things were explained properly, that there was no room for doubt and confusion. Which brought him back to the here and now. He was daring to believe that all was not hopeless, but there were still important things that he and Ruth had to discuss.

Ducking under the water, he caught her by surprise and drew her into his arms. They bobbed back to the surface, their legs tangling, her sleek body fitting snugly against his.

'My very own mermaid.' With the fingers of one hand he tucked some stray strands of wet hair back behind her ear. 'You lured me to my doom the first moment I looked at you, *sirena mia.*'

'Rico…'

Unable to help himself, he kissed her. He could do this all day and all night, he sighed, but he could not put off the inevitable any longer. 'We need to talk.'

'OK,' she agreed, but he felt some tension return to her body, and a flicker of anxiety dimmed some of the laughter in her eyes.

'From the very beginning, before we even met in person, I was in awe of your talent. Since then I have seen firsthand what an incredible doctor you are,' he told her, smiling at the hint of a blush that stained her cheeks. 'All along I wanted you to work for me. Seeing you at the clinic, you have exceeded all my expectations.'

Ruth licked her lips, distracting him, but as she went to speak, he stopped her.

'Please, I need to finish,' he stated, knowing he had to lay everything on the line for her.

'Go on,' she invited, curiosity and caution vying for prominence in her expression.

Rico sucked in a breath, knowing that the risk he was about to take was huge and could ruin everything. 'What has happened between us has changed things,' he continued, noting the frown that knotted her brow.

'Changed things how?'

'This is no longer just about the job.' Rico swallowed. Ruth's wariness was increasing his doubts and his nerves. 'The offer to work at the clinic comes with a condition.'

It was Ruth's turn to swallow. He saw the movement of her throat, the beat of her pulse, and her voice was more guarded when she spoke. 'What condition?'

'You can have the job, but you have to have *me*, as well. It's a package deal.' He faltered, his own heart thudding. 'I love you, Ruth, and I want you to be my wife.'

Something flared in her eyes, but she turned her head away before he could identify it. She slipped out of his arms and floated away, the dim light before dawn making it difficult to read her expression and gauge what she was thinking. Rico was scared. He had just taken the biggest gamble of his life. He knew Ruth, knew her body and soul, but could he win her heart? He also knew about her past, about those who had let her down and had not loved her as they should, and as she deserved. He wanted to give her all that love and support, and a family she'd never had. But how did she feel? She would never have given herself to him casually or on a whim. What they had shared had to have meant *something* to her—but what? Could she come to love him even a tiny bit as much as he loved her? He would do all he could to make her happy, to be worthy of her and her love.

His heart was in his mouth as he waited for her reply. He felt sick with worry. Had he just made another major mistake? He had risked every-thing, opened his heart for her and left it exposed, and he had never felt so vulnerable. Was she going to break his heart—or make him the happiest man alive?

Rico loved her!

Ruth hugged the knowledge to her, scarcely able to believe everything he had just said. She floated on her back, staring up at the inky-dark sky, trying to remember how to breathe. Rico came with the job. As her husband. He wanted her in every way. At work and at home. Partners in the fullest sense of the word.

Being with him made her feel good. In a very short time Rico had healed the wounds of her past and had made her feel whole and complete for the first time. He had not only taught her much about medicine, he'd taught her a lot about herself, too. He had given her new confidence, had openly believed in her. Instead of running her down like her parents did, undermining her, making her feel as if she was never good enough for anything, Rico heaped praise upon her, supported and encouraged her, welcomed her opinions, shared her joys and stood beside her to hold her up when things were difficult. And she was gaining so much…not just Rico, who was the centre of her world, but his family, too. A family who, in ten days, had shown her more love and kindness than her own had in her whole life.

She had not only found her true calling in her career, but she'd found her true love and her true home. With Rico. For the very first time in her life she felt as if she belonged, as if she mattered, as if she was worth something. He saw the person inside and loved every part of her, not at all intimidated by her brains. He cherished her, encouraged her, challenged her.

Somehow fate had conspired to bring them together in the most inexplicable and coincidental of ways, but she didn't care how it had happened, just that it had. She couldn't wait to tell Gina, who could soon be practically her sister by marriage, as well as her best friend. And then there was Holly. A moment of sadness intruded. How she wished that Holly, the last of their little circle to find love, could come to feel as happy as she did right at this moment.

Realising that Rico was waiting for her answer, she turned onto her front and slowly swam back to him. She looked into his melting hazel eyes with their intriguing gold speckles and saw his fear, his vulnerability. Her heart swelled with love for him. And with gratitude that he'd had the courage to open himself so completely, making her brave enough to do the same. That his whole world depended on what she said was written clearly in his eyes. She felt humbled by the knowledge of just how much he loved her. As she loved him. Completely. Inexorably. For ever.

'OK.' She struggled to keep her smile hidden. 'If that's the condition, I'll have to accept it.'

He looked less than happy, and she felt guilty for teasing him. 'You want the job that badly?'

'No. This isn't about the job. I want *you* that badly, Rico,' she told him, laughing as her meaning sank in and relief and pure joy radiated from him. 'I love you so much.'

Then she was back in his arms. She met and matched the passion of his kiss, tears of happiness spilling down her cheeks.

'You are in big trouble now,' he warned her, mischief in his eyes as he yet again lifted her up and headed for the steps at the corner of the pool. 'You nearly gave me heart failure, torment-ing me like that.'

The first streams of light were touching the eastern horizon as Rico carried her back towards his bedroom, but Ruth was too distracted to notice anything going on in the wider world. All that mattered was Rico—and them, here, together, sealing their bond.

'We're dripping water everywhere. The sheets will get wet,' she pointed out.

'I don't care.' She giggled as he dropped her on the bed, then followed her down and into her open arms. 'The steam we generate will soon dry things out,' he teased, then grew serious. 'I only care about you.'

Fresh tears beaded her lashes. 'I can't believe you love me,' she whispered, her voice throaty with emotion.

'I loved you from the first moment I saw you, *sirena mia*, and I have loved you more every day since. As I will for the rest of our lives. The men in our family are blessed that way—when we meet our one special woman, we know. As Papà did with Mamma, and Seb did with Gina. Now it is my turn…with you.'

The tears she had held in check, now spilled free. 'I love you, too.'

'I know there are things we have to work out,' he said, gently wiping the tracks of moisture from her cheeks. 'You will have to work out your notice?'

'Yes. It's three months,' she told him with a grimace.

He dropped a kiss on her nose. 'Do not worry. I have been thinking. I will change my schedule to leave Monday mornings and Friday afternoons free. Then I can fly over and spend the weekends with you—or you can come here when you are not on duty—and the time will soon pass.'

'You have been planning.'

'I had to believe my dreams might come true,' he told her, choking her up once more. 'I know you will miss Gina and Holly, but we will visit, and they can come to us any time. Do you think you will be happy here? As soon as I saw your house, I had hope you would like mine.'

She rested a palm against his face, needing to touch, loving the caress of his roguish stubble against her skin. 'I *love* it. Just today I told your mother and Emanuela how comfortable I was here and that I could never see all I want to in a lifetime. But what is important is being with you. I will be happy wherever you are,' she reassured him, meaning every word.

His own eyes looked suspiciously damp and his voice was rough with emotion. 'Thank you for making my world a better place. I will spend the rest of my life showing you how much I love and respect and cherish you, *sirena mia*.'

Ruth didn't think there was any way she could force words past the restriction in her throat, but Rico obligingly kissed her and prevented her from the need to try. She wrapped her arms around him and kissed him back with everything in her, re-igniting the fire of their passion, a passion she hoped would never be extinguished.

It was as if she had been reborn when she had met Rico. As if her life had only truly begun when fate had brought him to her, giving her meaning, fulfilling her not only on a professional level but making her whole as a woman. Adam's words no longer had the power to hurt. Rico had helped her to see them for what they were…lies. And with Rico she had blossomed into a sensual woman, confident in her power to satisfy and arouse and please her man, secure in his love for her and hers for him.

She had been scared to venture out of her comfort zone but Rico had led her from the darkness into the light and had taught her how special love was when you met the person with whom you bonded in your heart, soul and body. His belief in her was absolute, as was hers in him. Their bond was strong and theirs was a love to last a lifetime.

Her sexy Italian doctor had answered her call when she had emailed for help. He had more than delivered. He had changed her life. And now he offered her a future, one they would walk together, side by side—a future in which she was fulfilled and enriched, loved and cherished. His was a proposal that made her dreams come true and she was more than happy to accept.

MEDICAL™

Large Print

Titles for the next six months…

May

COUNTRY MIDWIFE, CHRISTMAS BRIDE	Abigail Gordon
GREEK DOCTOR: ONE MAGICAL CHRISTMAS	Meredith Webber
HER BABY OUT OF THE BLUE	Alison Roberts
A DOCTOR, A NURSE: A CHRISTMAS BABY	Amy Andrews
SPANISH DOCTOR, PREGNANT MIDWIFE	Anne Fraser
EXPECTING A CHRISTMAS MIRACLE	Laura Iding

June

SNOWBOUND: MIRACLE MARRIAGE	Sarah Morgan
CHRISTMAS EVE: DOORSTEP DELIVERY	Sarah Morgan
HOT-SHOT DOC, CHRISTMAS BRIDE	Joanna Neil
CHRISTMAS AT RIVERCUT MANOR	Gill Sanderson
FALLING FOR THE PLAYBOY MILLIONAIRE	Kate Hardy
THE SURGEON'S NEW-YEAR WEDDING WISH	Laura Iding

July

POSH DOC, SOCIETY WEDDING	Joanna Neil
THE DOCTOR'S REBEL KNIGHT	Melanie Milburne
A MOTHER FOR THE ITALIAN'S TWINS	Margaret McDonagh
THEIR BABY SURPRISE	Jennifer Taylor
NEW BOSS, NEW-YEAR BRIDE	Lucy Clark
GREEK DOCTOR CLAIMS HIS BRIDE	Margaret Barker

™ MILLS & BOON®

MEDICAL™

Large Print

August

EMERGENCY: PARENTS NEEDED	Jessica Matthews
A BABY TO CARE FOR	Lucy Clark
PLAYBOY SURGEON, TOP-NOTCH DAD	Janice Lynn
ONE SUMMER IN SANTA FE	Molly Evans
ONE TINY MIRACLE…	Carol Marinelli
MIDWIFE IN A MILLION	Fiona McArthur

September

THE DOCTOR'S LOST-AND-FOUND BRIDE	Kate Hardy
MIRACLE: MARRIAGE REUNITED	Anne Fraser
A MOTHER FOR MATILDA	Amy Andrews
THE BOSS AND NURSE ALBRIGHT	Lynne Marshall
NEW SURGEON AT ASHVALE A&E	Joanna Neil
DESERT KING, DOCTOR DADDY	Meredith Webber

October

THE NURSE'S BROODING BOSS	Laura Iding
EMERGENCY DOCTOR AND CINDERELLA	Melanie Milburne
CITY SURGEON, SMALL TOWN MIRACLE	Marion Lennox
BACHELOR DAD, GIRL NEXT DOOR	Sharon Archer
A BABY FOR THE FLYING DOCTOR	Lucy Clark
NURSE, NANNY…BRIDE!	Alison Roberts

millsandboon.co.uk Community

Join Us!

The Community is the perfect place to meet and chat to kindred spirits who love books and reading as much as you do, but it's also the place to:

- Get the inside scoop from authors about their latest books
- Learn how to write a romance book with advice from our editors
- Help us to continue publishing the best in women's fiction
- Share your thoughts on the books we publish
- Befriend other users

Forums: Interact with each other as well as authors, editors and a whole host of other users worldwide.

Blogs: Every registered community member has their own blog to tell the world what they're up to and what's on their mind.

Book Challenge: We're aiming to read 5,000 books and have joined forces with The Reading Agency in our inaugural Book Challenge.

Profile Page: Showcase yourself and keep a record of your recent community activity.

Social Networking: We've added buttons at the end of every post to share via digg, Facebook, Google, Yahoo, technorati and de.licio.us.

www.millsandboon.co.uk